Praise for
It's Gone Dark Over Bill's Mother's

'The title says it all. Close up and personal yet universal stories of childhood yearning, misunderstandings, loss and triumph. Beautifully written from inside, real people, ordinary homes. Set pieces, hilarious and tragic, the caravan site, the spring cleaning, the drinking game, crafted to perfection, short stories, to die for.' —Kit de Waal

'She picks the roofs off people's houses, then the tops off their minds and delves into the innermost heartaches and eccentricities of all of those diverse and beautiful and terrible human beings whose stories we hardly ever hear.'
—Hollie McNish

'Her stories combine the laugh-out-loud funny of Alan Bennett and the achingly sad of the great David Constantine.'
—Paul McVeigh

'Look out for this. With a sharp eye and tough warmth, Lisa Blower brings to life the silent histories and harsh realities of those living on the margins.' —*Shropshire Star*

over BILL'S MOTHER'S

IT'S GONE DARK

LISA BLOWER

First published in 2019 by
Myriad Editions
www.myriadeditions.com

Myriad Editions
An imprint of New Internationalist Publications
The Old Music Hall, 106–108 Cowley Rd, Oxford OX4 1JE

First printing
1 3 5 7 9 10 8 6 4 2

A CIP catalogue record for this book
is available from the British Library

ISBN (pbk): 978-1-912408-16-0
ISBN (ebk): 978-1-912408-17-7

Designed and typeset in Palatino
by WatchWord Editorial Services, London

Printed and bound in Great Britain
by Clays Ltd, Elcograf S.p.A.

For my two Nells—
from one storyteller to the next

Contents

Barmouth

Leek New Road, Stoke-on-Trent

THE CAR WAS second-hand: a Triumph Herald soft-top the colour of my daddy's overalls. He would drive, Mummy sitting aside of him in the passenger seat surrounded by food: barley sugars on the dashboard, sandwiches and flasks at her feet—it was the only time she was ever thankful for being short. She'd be knackered by the time she buckled herself in—baggy-eyed, short-tempered, hair rush-dyed with a home-snipped fringe—she'd been packing and shopping for weeks, filling up a box on the kitchen floor marked 'holiday'. I'd look down on it and think, when I grow up I won't be nothing like you. We'll eat fish and chips twice a week.

On the back seat were Nanny and Grandy Jack, Grandy Jack's chest wheezing like a burglar alarm. Nanny would press a fiver in my hand for holiday spends and make a big deal out of it, say, 'I know it's not much but we give you what we can,' and that chocolate would rot my teeth.

Then there was my sister. Four years younger, prettier and carsick, she'd be passed around the car to perch on knees. Every year we'd squabble over the caravan's top bunk and every year I'd be told, 'It's Looby's turn.' But she was even carsick on top bunk.

As for me, I'd been fashioned a bench from a plank of wood that slotted in behind the front seat. I'd spend the first half of the journey sitting astride of the handbrake navigating—'Second left at the roundabout', and '33 miles to Shrewsbury'—as if Daddy had never been down this road before.

The Amoco

We'd get going and stop five minutes later for petrol.

Why didn't you fill up last night?

Jen's on the till, isn't she?

Dad would ask, 'Does anyone want any chocolate?' and we'd watch him chatting with Jen on the till. Jen would wave. Aunty Jen. Sweet-toothed Jen. Nice as you like then she'd blow up like a chip-pan fire. 'Whatever's she done with her hair?' Nan would say, and Mum would tell us that Jen was going Majorca in a fortnight—all six of them, taking her mother, self-catering, only went Greece back in May—and then she'd stare out of the windscreen, her eyes filled with tears.

Dad would be back with a bagful of chocolate—Bounty, Mars Bars, Fry's Chocolate Cream bought special for Mum. 'Jen's looking well,' he'd say. 'Done something lovely with her hair,' and he'd get *the face*. 'For God's sake,' he'd mutter, pulling out of the forecourt, 'we're going on holiday, aren't we?' and we'd finally get on our way.

William Hill's

We'd have gone less than a mile before we'd pull in at the bookies. The men would get out and Mum would say to her mother, 'Can you believe this? Now, do you see? *Do you see?*'
But it might pay for the holiday.
Get the girls something nice to wear.
Just think, we could all be going Majorca next year.
We're all off to sunny Spain.
But you never win.
Mug's game.
I'm the bloody mug.
Yeah well, you know what you can do, don't you?
And as the car door slammed shut, Nan would start to tell us the story about the two little girls—one who had a posh pram and one who had a rusty one whose wheel fell off and rolled into the pond.

Loggerheads

Just past Loggerheads and my sister would be sick on the verge. Mum would be with her, holding her hair up in the air, and shouting at the car.
It's the way you drive, like it's some race track.
You took that last corner on two wheels.
One sat on our knees, the other on a plank. We'll get stopped one day. The police will have us, and then what? *Then what?* I'm pig sick of making do!
And Dad swivels round in the driving seat and says to me, 'Have I ever told you how I met your mum in Loggerheads?'
He has. A million times.

'She was on the back of another man's motorbike swigging from a bottle of sweet sherry and her hair was as dark as treacle. It was love at first sight,' though he's not looking at my mum when he says it. He's looking down at his Mars Bar, his stomach lurching at Jen's fingerprints on the wrapper.

My sister gets back in the car. Dad fiddles with the car radio. Fleetwood Mac. *I want to be with you everywhere.* We'd sing. We'd get back on our way. Mum reaching over to put a hand on Dad's thigh. She pats his leg in time to the music. He flinches. She moves her hand away and makes a bony little fist she cannot use.

Ford, just outside of Shrewsbury on the A458

We called it dinner—meat-paste sandwiches, salt-your-own crisps, apples and pears and what was left of the chocolate. We'd sit in the lay-by, taking it in turns to wee behind the hedge. We'd have left the house almost two hours ago. Mum would be looking as if she'd walked there. There'd be dents on her knees from where the cooler box had been. I say, 'If we stopped for fish and chips you wouldn't have to carry the picnic on your knees.'

Me and my mum: we become our own worst enemies and yet each other's only friend.

Or, Montford Bridge off the A5

We should call and see Aunty Bobby. She'd love to see the girls.

But they're in their holiday clothes.

What does that matter?

They'll be covered in dog hairs. Filled up on biscuits. That woman will be there. You know I don't like it in front of the girls.

Why do you have to be like that? If it wasn't for Aunty Bobby and her caravans!

Do you hear that, Mother? Married beneath him, he has. As if I need reminding.

We don't take the turning to Aunty Bobby's and carry on.

Dinas Mawddwy

We'd see the road sign and hold our breath.

You should've gone through Bala.

You do this every year.

The car's too old for the hill.

What do you want to prove?

The car can't take it. *I can't take it!*

Dad would shove the car into first gear, an eight-car tailback chugging behind. He'd crunch into second. It'd labour. It'd be quicker for us to pick it up, walk with it. He'd put the car back into first. The car behind us would toot, flash its lights, start to pull out.

Lord, give me strength! We're all going to die!

There'd be a funny smell coming from the engine, like the front wheels were coming away. Dad would stare straight ahead, and shift into third gear.

First one to see the sea!

He always did want a bit better. Always did ache to overtake.

Tal-y-bont

Three miles outside of Barmouth, and Looby is sick again. We all get out of the car to stretch our legs.

'Look at the colour of that sky,' says Mum, and orders Dad to get the camera. He asks where it is. 'Wherever you put it,' she says.

'Didn't you pack it?' he asks, and Mum closes her eyes.

'I ask you to do nothing but pack the camera, fill up the night before.'

I now know why we never have any holiday snaps.

'Just go!' Mum yells at Dad. 'You don't want to be here. For crying out loud, I don't want to be here.'

'This isn't about *Barmouth*!'

Nan ushers us back into the car. Let them argue in peace. Me and Looby crouch under the headlamps and count the dead insects. She takes the right, I take the left, the one with the most dead on their lamp wins.

Barmouth

It's 1982, around five o'clock. We're at war with Argentina. My dad hasn't yet been called up. He's waiting. The sparkies are next, he says. They'll need sparkies to rewire the guns, keep the power running through the sockets. Grandad tells him to shut up. He doesn't know what he's talking about. You've no idea what war does to a man. Dad says that's exactly the point. He *wants* to feel like a man.

Mum thumps his shoulder and tells him to shut up. She says if he got called up he'd shit himself and bend every rule in the book not to go.

We drive along the promenade in silence until Nan says, 'It's gone downhill.'

'It looks the same as last year to me.'

'And the year before that, and the year before that.'

I see all the things that haven't changed and cheer at each one. The black spindle towers of the railway bridge, the flags at the top of the helter-skelter, the neon lights of the prize bingo, the Shell Shop where I'd buy gifts for schoolfriends, the Smuggler's Rest where I'd be allowed scampi, adult portion, and cheesecake.

We pull into the car park by the beach. I hope it's for ice cream, a cone of chips, but no. Grandad's legs have gone dead again. Nan has to rub at his shins. Mum sprays Ralgex. We all cough. I turn around, straddle the bench the other way, and start to help. Grandad pushes me away. 'You're too old for that,' he warns.

Mum's face reddens. 'Do you realise how that sounds?' she shouts. 'Can this family show no one any affection?'

Dad opens the car door but doesn't actually leave the car. He just sighs. Then he sighs again. When I look at Mum she's crying. That's the fourth time today. There'll be a fifth and sixth time before she goes to bed and then in the morning she'll bustle about the kitchen frying up as if nothing is wrong with us at all.

Gwyn Evans's Caravan Site

Grandad asks for a different inhaler. The one that jump-starts his breath. He says he can't feel his right foot and his chest heaves like a tired racehorse. We pull up at their caravan first. Dad carries in their cases. Grandad sits on the step of the caravan, wheezing. Nan steps over him. 'We've only just got here and look at the state of you!' but Grandad has no clean breath left. Mum tells him to breathe in the sea air. It'll do him good. He does as she says but we all know that nothing can do him much good any more; fifty years of pot-banks fogging up his lungs.

Nan's in the caravan making tea, making the bed, bleaching the toilet, disinfecting the sinks. She tells Mum they'll be over once they've had a brew and unpacked. 'You can grill that gammon,' she says. 'I'll peel some spuds once I've washed my feet.'

Every year, the same blue bowl, bunions soothed, spuds peeled.

Golygfa Glân

It means beautiful view, or the view is beautiful. Either way, we can see the sea out of every window. I lie on top bunk and listen to the rain. It hammers down like hailstones on the roof and makes the gas bottles sing. Looby is asleep. Dad has gone down the site pub for a swifty with Roger from the caravan next door. Roger comes up from Solihull with his wife Charmaine every weekend. He sells cars, second-hand ones, and car accessories like ice scrapers and hub polish that Charmaine sells from the caravan hatch. He keeps telling Dad that if he doesn't branch out on his own he'll get left behind—be your own boss, cook your own books, life's going to get a lot more selfish, squire—and as he laughs like a drain down his ear, he offers Dad a good price for the Triumph he doesn't take.

Mum and Charmaine kiss each other hello but they don't mean it. Charmaine goes about in a bikini and raffia wedge heels with matching handbag. Mum covers up because the sun burns her skin and she has to lie down on her front while one of us dots her back with calamine lotion. Before Dad went to the pub, he said, 'The girls are fine. They know where we are. Ask your mother over if you're that worried. And we are on holiday, love. One drink won't hurt.'

There was a lot of quiet before my mum seethed through gritted teeth that 'this is never a holiday for me.'

Barmouth beach

It's 1984. The miners are striking back home. My dad is not a miner but he works at the colliery, tinkering, as my mum calls it, with the wires and fuse boxes that keep the lifts going up and down the shafts. He is not striking. He says we live hand to mouth as it is and if he strikes, what will happen to the men who want to work if the lift stops working? Mum says, 'It's going to close whether you like it or not.'

We all lie on Barmouth beach hemmed in by windbreaks and sunbathing on pebbles. My sister's making sand pies. Rhubarb and custard, chicken and ham, the shells she collects in her bucket are the spuds and peas on the side. Grandad snoozes in a deckchair, his breathing rugged and raspy, an old raggedy cowboy paperback going up and down on his chest. Nan is sitting aside of him covered head to toe in blankets doing a word search. Brrr, she goes, and Brrr just in case. 'I told you we should have come last week,' she moans. 'Blazing sunshine last week.'

'Yes,' snarls Mum. 'The weather is all my fault too.' And she looks across at my dad who looks out to sea and says, 'There's got to be somewhere better than this.'

He picks up my sister's spade and starts to dig in the sand like a dog.

The Smuggler's Rest

A year later and we come in August for a change, as if the time of year will make the place different. It is not. We go to the Smuggler's Rest and my sister is sick in three napkins. She'd been allowed the scampi then had had the peach melba. The waiter brings us the bill. Mum gasps. 'We don't have enough cash.' She roots in her handbag, asks Dad, 'Have you got the cheque book?'

'Why would I bring the cheque book?'

'We haven't brought the cheque book?'

'Well, *I* didn't bring the cheque book.'

'You didn't think to bring the cheque book?'

And they still don't look at each other in case the other turns to stone.

After the strikes didn't work and the men lost their jobs, Dad took what he could and went in the office. Paper-shuffling, my nan calls it. Head of paperclips, sarks my mum. Keeping a roof over our heads, shouts Dad. We don't get pocket money any more and we pay for everything with the cheque book.

Nan pipes up, 'Well, just how short are you?'

Mum says it's embarrassing. 'We're £12 short.' She looks down at Nan's handbag.

'Don't even think about it,' says Nan.

'But you get a free holiday, every year, and it's only £12. We'll pay you back.'

'I know you will, we're pensioners.' Nan asks for my purse too. 'I know you haven't spent it,' she says.

My mum's mouth drops open. 'You're not seriously taking her holiday money?'

Nan folds her arms and tells me that like the little girl with the rusty pram and the wonky wheel, if you want something nice you've either got to pay for it or go without.

I remember that I got out my fiver. It looked so expensive in my hand. Mum cried and left the restaurant. I watched her go and felt sad. She looked so small, like she'd fit in my Nan's handbag, and she'd tried, she'd really tried, but I was sad mainly because I wished I'd had the peach melba. It was so much bigger than the cheesecake. When we came back two years later, without Dad and by taxi, the Smuggler's Rest was a Chinese takeaway.

Swallow Falls

I'm fifteen and reading a book, swotting up for my GCSEs. I don't remember the book. I'm mediocre in everything, shine in nothing, and certainly not up there with my sister whose art is already winning prizes. Mum calls out, 'Oi, bookworm, get yourself off up that hill, get the blood flowing, some fresh air in your lungs!'

I carry on reading. I've been up that hill fourteen times. I can draw the view in my mind, tell you what shade of green goes where. They trudge off and leave me with Grandad parked up on a rock. He says, 'How's school?'

I think about the girls who don't speak to me. The one who says I copy her hair. The teacher who tells me I upset people, especially the girl with the demi-wave and the Russian wedding ring on her engagement finger. He tells me, 'You know she hasn't got a dad, so why are you so mean?' I tell him I'm not mean. My dad left too and they make things up. I ask them, 'What is it that I've done to you?' They say, 'If you don't know then we're not going to tell you,' and I hide in the toilets, punching at the spots that are ruining my face. Nor do I tell him that I've already done it with Christian Davis because the girl with the demi-wave is doing it with Robbie Hannan, or that I've had a persistent sickness bug since May and no bleed.

'Fine,' I tell Grandad, 'school's fine,' and carry on reading the book.

Shell Island

I squint in the sunshine at the dunes. I can't remember why I used to beg to come here—sand in the sandwiches, sand in your eyes—most people my age are in Benidorm, Ibiza, Florida, Cornwall. 'Where the fuck's Barmouth?' the girls snide. 'Sounds like a shit-hole to me.'

I think about all those coral necklaces I used to buy them from the Shell Shop. Those little pebble egg-timers, the dead starfish and pieces of sponge I'd buy as bathroom trinkets. I wonder if anybody actually kept them. Why no one ever bought me presents back from Disneyland or sent me a postcard from St Ives. I wonder how they're all getting on at Sixth Form College without me, whether any of them care for what it's like to have a baby and let it go without even knowing whether it was a boy or girl. My nan said that way was for the best.

After their divorce, Mum remarried quickly. Registry office, pub grub, dress from Dorothy Perkins Petite section. We weren't bridesmaids. It wasn't that kind of wedding and we didn't know most of the guests. Nan didn't come either. They still weren't speaking at the time. Mum had to give herself away. I said, 'What about a friend? Don't you have a friend who could do it?' But after she slapped me across the face, I realised that Mum doesn't have any friends. She finds a man and lives through him instead.

My step-dad is called Trevor. *Trefor*. She met him at the site pub the year after Dad left, but we know that's not true. Trefor was always the one who did the odd jobs on the caravan. The handyman. *Tasgmon*. Trefor pays for everything with ten-pound notes, but he's never got any change when the ice-cream van comes tinkling its bell round the estate.

I think about my dad back at home in his new flat. Turns out Jen never did feel the same way. He left anyway. Mum said, 'It was an affair in the head.' Dad said that wasn't true. For a minute or two he was really in love. We see him every Saturday and then every Wednesday night. We stop over on bunk beds that he has in his bedroom and he sleeps on the sofa in the front room. When we're not there he sleeps on bottom bunk. His feet hang over the end. The duvet covers him like a facecloth. He can only sleep on his side. He says he doesn't mind. He just pretends that he's sleeping in the bunk beds of Aunty Bobby's caravan. 'And I've always had a good night's sleep up Barmouth,' he says.

He makes sure we have a week in the caravan every year. He says it's important for us to get a break. He comes round the house the night before we go to fill up Trefor's Mini Metro at the Amoco. He leaves two Bounty bars in the glovebox and, sometimes, a Fry's Chocolate Cream for Mum as if this is enough to woo her back. It isn't and it doesn't. And if he doesn't put the petrol in, Mum and Trefor won't take us. They say we can't afford it.

My sister is up in the dunes sketching with gold crayons. Mum and Trefor are sat in a pair of deckchairs swigging from hipflasks, stroking hands. I go and check on Nan. She's been sat in the passenger seat of Trefor's Mini Metro for over an hour just staring out of the windscreen and clutching onto her handbag as if it were about to be snatched. She warns me every day—'The world's rotting. Never trust a man who can't put a penny between his eyes'—and I measure the distance between Trefor's eyes and wonder what they see in Mum.

I knock on the window and ask if she's OK. She looks at me. For a moment she doesn't know me and the grip on her handbag tightens. Then she remembers. She breaks out into a smile. She calls me by my sister's name. I don't correct her. It's good that she remembers one of us. I ask her if she wants an ice cream. She fishes in her purse and pushes a fiver through the gap in the window. 'Get your grandad a 99,' she says. 'I love to watch him licking raspberry ripple off his chin.'

I don't tell her that Grandad's been dead two years on Tuesday. I don't take the fiver either. Mum says that death can do funny things to a woman. 'She'll be out the other side come Christmas,' she says, coming towards the car. 'Any longer than that and she's just milking it for effect,' and she feeds my nan a couple of aspirin and opens a flask of tea.

93 Sharrow Lane

I live with a boy who likes a drink, likes the ladies, comes back to me when he's skint. I spread holiday brochures on the bed, count out my copper collection labelled 'holiday', and check what's left on my Visa. We watch Ceefax on the telly, holiday hotspots and last minute deals. 'We could go to Malta,' I say. 'Or stretch to Ibiza. How much have you got left on your Visa?'

He reaches for a can and says, 'Put your bikini on. I want to see you in a bikini.'

I do because I can't stop loving him and I want to be loved by someone like him.

Mum calls me later and tells me the caravan's free. I can have it first week of August and the forecast is good. 'But for God's sake take your sister,' she instructs. 'I'm up to here with her feminist crap!'

My sister's just finished her A levels. She's off to London to study Fine Art. She's just come back from Paris. One of her teachers paid for her to go. She's come home swooning. *Manon* this and *Manon* that. She says it's like they've met before in another life.

My boyfriend tells me he doesn't want to go to Barmouth. He doesn't know where it is but it sounds shit and he doesn't want to go with my lezzer of a sister either, and while we're at it, I'm done with you too. This is going nowhere. *You* are going nowhere.

'You're dumping me?' and I collapse on the bed panting, I can't get my breath, and he shrugs and says, 'Perhaps, it depends,' and starts to untie my bikini strings.

By the time we get to Barmouth, my sister's full of cold, and I'm single with cystitis. It rains all week. It hammers down on the caravan roof. I sit on the toilet sobbing and rolling fleas between my fingers, breaking their backs one by one.

We go to all the old places: Shell Island, Swallow Falls, the prize bingo. We eat Cup a Soups, mash up Bounty bars in black cherry yoghurt and huddle under the parasol to smoke. A caravan window opens across the way. 'I remember you two,' she says. 'Always a smile, always excited to be here, now look at you both,' and she shakes her head and snaps the window shut.

The next night, we take a table in the site pub as far away from the fruit machines as we can get and still Charmaine hunts us out. She totters over in leopard-skin and says, 'Divorce didn't buy you Majorca then?' and asks if we took a wrong turn at the airport. 'You two still coming to this squat?' she says, and she's either drunk or she's bored, we still can't work her out, and she starts to quiz Looby about her purple-rimmed glasses and pink and blonde hair, and then guffaws into her Cinzano, '*Lesbian.*'

Looby stands up to correct her. 'Actually, it's Louisa,' she snaps. 'And I'd rather live as *I want* than be like you living for man after man, because really Charmaine, you should charge for it,' but by this point, she's looking at me.

We go back to the caravan in silence. I open the door, open a can of lager, offer one to my sister and she says no, come on, we're done here, we're done, and then she adds, 'You need to sort yourself out now, because you know what you are, don't you? You're turning into Mum.'

She asks me to drive her home then. I refuse. So she calls a cab, catches the train and heads off to university with the clothes on her back and not a care in the world.

The Prize Bingo

I call Mum from the payphone in the amusement arcade. 'I'm going to come home,' I tell her. 'I need somewhere to clear my head.'

She says now's not such a good time. She's taken in a lodger. Step-Dad's a prick. Divorces are expensive. 'You'll like Alan,' she says. Got a dry-cleaning business apparently, stops Monday to Thursday night in my old bedroom and when he's not overloading her washer with his work shirts, he keeps on at her about a double bed. 'That's a thought,' she says. 'He could have mine.'

I put the phone down knowing that Alan doesn't sleep in the back bedroom any more. I call my dad. He lodges with a farmer now, the one who bought the land from Aunty Bobby before she died. He lives in an old bubble caravan in their backyard that reeks of pig-swill and chicken shit. He sounds just as sad on the phone. I tell him that old Mr Evans has stuck a note to the caravan door. That he's offered to tow the caravan off site for scrap but it'll cost. Says he's no place on his site for a caravan that rusty, and before I leave, he tapers ticker tape around the awning, its navy blue letters warning—*Dangerous*—to anyone who thinks it's not static. My dad tuts on the other end of the phone. 'What shall I do?' I ask.

Because gone are the days when I could leave it with him. I was sixteen when he got laid off at the colliery, eighteen when he had his breakdown and came out of it a crumpled crisp packet of a man, muscles disintegrated into the flat tyres and tired clutch pedals of the dead Triumph he clung onto for dear life and nostalgia and which now sits rusting in Aunty Bobby's backyard, part of the chicken coop and overrun with dead flies. He wears a pair of glum tatty eyes that only light up when he sees my mother, and his hands shake from the drink. He blames twenty years down the coalface but lift-shaft maintenance has still not made it onto the compensation lists. He says things like, 'if you don't put money into it, it'll die', and 'there's never any future if you've had your power cut'. I tell my dad I have nowhere to go. I tell him that I've got lost and surely he understands.

'I'm not making it up Dinas Mawddwy,' I say.

He offers me the left settee bunk of his caravan.

The pips run out before I decide.

In the end I call Nan. She's ninety-two now. She says I can have the camp bed. She'll put it up for me behind the settee. I cry when I see it. She says, 'That bed's only temporary so look at it and be determined.' And she gives me a fiver and tells me to go and get us fish and chips. The batter makes her sick and they're old potatoes, gone in the water. 'Nothing's like it used to be,' she complains. I tell her that Barmouth's not like it used to be either, that the caravan is on its last legs. Old Evans wants it towed off site. She scolds me for being ungrateful. 'Do you know what I'd give to go to Barmouth right now?' she says.

I don't tell her what I've done to the caravan. How I blame Barmouth for so much. That I'm awaiting the police to charge me with attempted arson. That I'm long past caring whether I serve time or not. That only Charmaine knows that I was trying to go down with it. How she later saves my bacon in court.

'Don't you want to see the world?' I ask my nan.

'But I have my world right here,' she says, and I'll never forget that look on her face: the same as it was when Mum found her in the armchair, drifted off to sleep with just a fiver in her purse.

75 Kielder Square

The council found us a two-bed flat and we've sold the car for peanuts. My daughter has just turned eight. She thinks sharing her bedroom with Grandma is fun.

Mum's at the door – eighty-one now, keys lost again, chocolate round her mouth, Morrison's carrier bag full of sun lotion.

'What have you been doing?' I shriek. 'Where've you been? I've been worried sick, about to call the police.'

I make her tea. Her hands are frozen and her feet have swelled. 'What have *you* been doing?' Mum asks me. 'Don't you go to work?'

I tell her again. Redundant, last October, both of us let go one after the other and we lost the house, negative equity, awful time with the bailiffs, so humiliating on the front lawn. He's gone to his mother's to think.

'You'll want this fiver, then,' she says. 'Your dad will never forgive me otherwise.'

I don't know what she's talking about. I tell her, 'You don't owe me £5 and you don't have any money.' And then because the doctors tell you to do so, I add, 'Dad's dead, Mum, so it doesn't matter.'

Mum looks crestfallen. She thought he was washing up.

'No, Mum. He's not washing up.'

She takes four bottles of sun lotion out of the carrier bag and tells me they're for the holiday box. I hand her tea and tell her there is no holiday box; no holiday either.

'I do,' she says, perking up. 'I owe you £5,' and she starts reminiscing.

I let her. You're supposed to. It makes her feel well, and I sit next to her and listen. It's an old favourite. The one about the holiday in Barmouth and how we ate at the Smuggler's Rest and didn't have enough for the bill. She doesn't remember where she's just been or that she and my nan kept up a stony silence for getting on three years after that; how that £12 could've been cited in my parents' divorce proceedings the humiliation was that raw, but she still remembers that she owes me a fiver.

Mum takes out her purse and fumbles through the compartments. I take the purse off her, she's all fingers and thumbs, and I notice that it's more photograph album than purse. I take out the photographs and lay them on the table. We laugh at them together. We're all on Barmouth beach, the sky is inky-black, the sea is raging yet we look so alive.

'Those holidays were lovely,' Mum says. 'I wouldn't change them for the world.'

I show the pictures to my daughter when she comes in from school. I listen to Mum tell my daughter how lucky she was. Then she returns everything to her purse and removes £5. I look at it shaking in her hand. It means as much to me now as it did back then.

No. It means more.

She gives it to my daughter. Tells her, 'I know it's not much but we give you what we can,' and not to spend it on chocolate. So I drink my tea and watch my daughter cuddle up against her, ask if she'll tell her the story about the two little girls: one who had a posh pram and one who had a rusty one and what happened when the wheel fell off and rolled into the pond.

As Mum talks I look at my sister's painting on the wall. It's called 'Plank', dedicated to me, given to me for my fortieth birthday. Aside of it is another painting, 'Barmouth', a grubby-looking block of brown and raffia she's told me to sell. 'It'll get you back on your feet,' she says. 'And it's not as if it's a triumph.' 'Barmouth' is worth over thirty thousand pounds.

My mother's voice drifts back into earshot. 'So, you see, we all start off in a pram. It's only when we see what the other girls have that we want what they have and that's when things get rusty.'

I realise what *I'd* like to see more than anything in the world. I head towards the phone to finally make that call.

Pot Luck

WHAT CAN I GET YOU, duck? Sausage? Egg? Cup of tea? Don't worry. You're here now, so you can stop looking at the floor. I welcome all lids that don't fit and spouts that don't pour. Who told you about me? Though you look familiar, duck. Like I know you. Who's your mother? Does she live on Werrington Road? It's the eyes, you see. I never forget a pair of eyes and you've big eyes, duck. They give you away. I hope you don't mind me saying that, but eyes like yours are sad stories. You tell them whether you like it or not.

Come and get warm. That's it. You need some sugar in that tea—you're skin and bone—but I haven't got any. Food bank was that busy last week you forget what you need. *Do I not get to choose? Can I not get some of that? What am I supposed to do with kidney beans?* Her from number 9

21

chinning about the veg again: *I'd rather frozen if you've got it, duck. Those carrots last month went black.* I said to her, 'Next time you chuck stuff out chuck them to me. I can make meals out of onions.' She says, 'Well give us a fiver then and I'll see what's on the turn.' Course, some faces don't want you to see them. Make out like they don't know you when they sat aside of you in school. Others turn up with a couple of shopping trucks, next door's baby, and barefaced cheek. It's like there's a war on, rationing all over again. My mother would say, 'If there's men in the world there'll always be wars.' And my father would go, 'Hester. As long as there's women there'll be men and dunna forget that it only took one woman to bring down a lifetime of men.' And off he'd go again: *there was a time when you couldn't eat a meal in any decency without the potters from Stoke. Pride of every dinner table we were till those slow boats from China promised cheap, cheap, cheap. Can't grow a bloody teapot for toffee any more. Four thousand kilns gone later and it's gone that dark over Bill's mother's you realise just how much daylight those kilns let in.*

Saw everything through sad eyes did my father. Said they'd pulled the plug on Stoke while the likes of Manchester got rewired. 'Bright lasses want bright lights,' he'd say. But that was emigration as far as mother was concerned. Daughters should stay at home.

Have a sausage. Go on. It's on me. How long have you been like this? Sorry, that's your business. But I probably did. I probably knew your mother. Was she a redhead with glasses too big for her face? I used to know a lot of people round here but there's that many faces with their heads down now you don't get to know anyone like you used to. Dumping ground this road. Watched a sorry business only the other week. You'd think they'd have done it without fuss, but no. Blue flashing lights, three from the Social, kiddies crying—*Mama, Mama*—Ukraine, someone says. Next stop Dover. Some disused factory they'll get held in before they're shipped back. Makes you wonder. It's got to be bad where they're from to want to sneak in here. Blimey, is it dinnertime already? Hello, Benny. You're looking brighter. Had yourself a bit of sleep have you? It's sausage today, duck. Few mushrooms. No, that's fine. Fifty pence is grand. Just don't give all that butty to your dog. Me? Oh you know me, Benny, still waiting on the knee and our Keeley to call but you get ill if you dwell, don't you? You take care now. Ta-ra.

You won't believe me, but once upon a time he was one of the royal gilders was Benny. Only worked in gold leaf. Rumour has it he always worked with a penny in his shoe, keep his luck and a steady hand. Course, he got the boot like everyone else except he's gone and bought his house hasn't he? *My right to buy*, he says putting in a new conservatory, *and shrouds don't come with purses*. Next thing you know, he owes more than he's borrowed and he's down the bookies trying win the repayments, then takes to the booze on the never-never. Says he'd rather learn to limp than take that penny from his shoe because one day his luck will change. Won't tell me his real name. Says that's the only thing he's got left worth something. I call him Benny. Otherwise he's just another one of them that you don't know by name but by how long they've been on the dole. Come to the window. Let me show you out here. See him? Fourteen months. And then him, with that tartan trolley? You can tell by the way he won't look you in the eye that it's been almost five years. No one wants them you see. Nothing doing. And her, with all those carrier bags? She's spent longer out here than she ever has in a house. Slipped through the net. Forgotten about. Can't remember what it's like to matter when all self-worth's been bound in paid employment, yet she won't have you fussing her. Not when there's nowt in those carrier bags but pride.

What about a toastie? Let me do you a toastie. I've got a bit of cheese left. I'll slice this onion. Let me tell you this: I had a big life once. He were a big brute in the end, but it was a big do, a big day, we even went Barbados and came back to a big house, new baby on the way an' all; and I tell it like this because it's supposed to be a big society, isn't it? But then his big job went, ping went the big dreams, and the big house got sold at a bargain-bin rate. Then he goes and leaves me and the baby for some broad who'd been growing bigger in secret and I find out that all that big debt of his was in a joint account. I remember standing in the shop, shortly after he left, seven pence short of a split bag of rice. *Seven pence short of a split bag of rice.* That's when you start to think you'd rather die than ask the big queue behind you for a bit of small change.

Anyhow. The council finds us a house. Except our Keeley—that's my daughter by the way, and she'll be eighteen next week you know? Eighteen! I've got her this bracelet, let me show you. You can try it on. She's got thin wrists like you. Look at that! It fits a treat. Anyway. Our Keeley leaves home at sixteen. Thinks she's in love and he loves her and next thing I know, someone from the council comes to see me. Handsome devil, didn't tuck his shirt in, wouldn't take a cup of tea. Says according to new laws I've been doing a family-in-need out of a home. 'Under-occupying', he calls it. Reads me the riot act then shows me a stack of grainy pictures on his computer of this place and that, no room to swing a cat. All meters and storage heaters and a two-bar gas-effect fire. I thought to myself, someone's been on the snitch here, so I said to him, 'Who've you been talking to, duck?'

He said, 'It's a period of review, Mrs Johnson. Time to discuss your options.'

I said, 'I thought the point of paying in taxes was so you could get summat back from the state when you really needed it.'

He said, 'Have you got any savings, Mrs Johnson? Anything you've not let on about?'

I said, 'I've not a bean, duck. Why would I when you know I'm still paying off my husband's debts?'

He said, 'Well, we'd better get things moving then because these homes today are pot luck.'

I said, 'What about my daughter? What if she wants to come home?'

But he's on his mobile chinning away and telling me I can move in end of the month.

Course, they shift me that quick I can hardly get my bearings and it's as damp as dishcloths in here. I'll have pneumonia soon: summat bronchial I'll be put on another list for. No beds in hospitals, no houses available. Waiting lists as long as both arms. My mother always said that we'd queue for a cod's head if they said on the telly there were no fish in the sea. Only got to look at how we went queuing for petrol. Folk like us are a government's bread and butter. We bankroll the rich whether we like it or not. Take this place. Not council, not social, but private. And that means a landlord who'd skin a gnat for its hind and it's all run on greedy-guts meters that keep the shareholders warm as toast. Take the phone. It guzzles pound coins. Though I don't think my daughter gave me her right number.

Where did you live, duck? I knew your mother didn't I? From Werrington Road. What happened? Whatever it's about, it's not worth it. Take me and our Keeley. Always so angry and rushing through life. Says, 'It's my life, Mam. Not yours to have a second chance at'—and that there's no company car to be had in making butties. Going to be an optician she was. 'You want eyes in the back of your head round here,' she'd say. 'What with you feeding the five thousand and everyone on the take.'

I said, 'I don't ever see you helping anyone out. I could rent your room out the amount of time you spend on the lash or holed up with whatever bloke catches your eye.'

And she goes, 'Well now I know how you really see me,' and I haven't clapped eyes on her since.

It's her birthday soon. Did I say? I've got her a bracelet. Bake her a nice cake.

Oh here comes trouble! Blimey, Mickey! What's happened to you? Is that blood? Use the bathroom, wash your face. Shall I do you a butty? I've a rasher of bacon left. I could fry you an egg. You're probably too young to remember this, but you used to go to work on an egg. That's right. *Go to work on an egg.* What did you call me? Cooped up mother-hen? You want to watch it, sunshine. You've already had one thump today and too many eggs give you boils. Go on then. Take that bit of cake with you. See you tomorrow. Ta-ra.

He's a rum bugger is Mickey. No family to speak of and all of a wander. One of them kids, you know? In and out of care then in and out of cells. If it wasn't for me he'd starve. But like I say, who wants to cook a meal for one every day? It's not illegal and I'm doing nothing wrong. I'm needed, that's all. *Needed.* And we all need our daily bread.

Have you finished, duck? I'm not on the take but I'd be grateful for a pound for the phone to call my daughter if you've got it. No. Thirty pence is thirty pence. Look after the pennies and it all adds up. You've got a bit of fuel inside you now so remember: the road goes up, not just down, and it goes left and right. You know where I am now so call again. Ta-ra. Keep safe.

Hey! Hang on minute. You've got our Keeley's bracelet! Hey! Come back! Stop her, someone! Damn these bloody crutches and my knees! Please, someone! Tell her to come back. You there! Are you listening? I need your help.

Broken Crockery

MUM SAYS MY NAN'S in hospital with Margaret Thatcher. She said she'd tripped over the hearthrug and broke her arm by smashing it on the fireplace. I've never liked that fireplace. I don't like that china sausage dog that stares at me like I'm teasing it with something tasty in my pocket. When my nan's not looking I hide it in the bin. Nan says that sausage dog is the last of the Potteries. It deserves to be on show to make everyone remember what this place was. Mum says that when Nan fell, she broke the sausage dog's legs. Mum says bones get brittle. Sometimes, she says, they don't even mend. I asked if my nan's bones would mend. Mum said Margaret Thatcher could pay for new ones. That sausage dog is lying on its belly in our bin. Its legs are covered in teabags and burnt fruitcake.

My nan doesn't like Margaret Thatcher because she'd kicked women in the shins and blew off kneecaps so a working man would know what mercy meant. She said that Margaret Thatcher drove a tank straight through the poor people and was only wearing a headscarf. She said that Margaret Thatcher said that everyone should have a house because that was the law. Mum says houses are greedy old things. They take up all your money and need new clothes all the time. I've bought my nan a new pair of slippers for her birthday. They're fashion ones, like my nan wants. My nan isn't old. She said in her head she's only thirty-three. 'How old is Margaret Thatcher?' I asked. 'The devil looks after its own,' said my nan.

Mum used to leave magazines open on the pages she wanted my dad to see, and stuck pictures of new ovens on the kitchen cupboards so he could see them when he made a cup of tea. I put a picture of a new telly there just in case. Nan says I should ask Margaret Thatcher for a new telly because that's what she's made the kids like today. Want, want, want, she says, they've got tellies in their bedrooms and chips on their laps and don't know what it is to have a good dinner or watch a proper telly show that isn't about murder or people acting up. Nan says kids don't talk any more, just write on computers. I said, 'I talk, Nan.' She said I don't count. 'You were born for a pot bank,' she said. 'But now we're a nation of salespeople. It used to be marvellous around here. Everyone was the same.' I said, 'What am I?' She said, 'You're different.' I said, 'No, I want to be a vet.'

Mum told me to give her a right big hug before she went to the hospital. 'What for?' I said. She said she needed it. I said I wanted to go too. She said I couldn't because the buses were scary in the dark. I pretended my arm was broken just like my nan's for a joke. Mum said, 'Broken bones aren't funny bones.' I said, 'Doctors mend bones. They have to.' Mum told me that some bones stay broken. 'Sometimes,' she said, 'broken bones are things like livers and kidneys.'

'Like in a pie?' I asked.

Mum said, 'Sometimes bones don't get better.'

'Like when you made that pie and you forgot about it in the oven and it all got burnt?' I said.

'And sometimes bones get buried,' she said.

'Like the dog in the bin?' I asked.

'Sometimes you can't heal bones,' she said.

'Yes, you can,' I said. 'If doctors can't mend them, God does. He makes up a big bed in the healing room.'

'Who told you that?' she said.

'Nan did,' I said.

'And what else did your nan tell you?' she said.

'That she's too pretty to die,' I said.

Mum said I should make Nan a card that said 'Get Well Nan, come home soon'. I got out my felt-tips and drew my nan at the bingo. She wouldn't want me to draw her in bed with a thermometer in her mouth. She'd rather have a fag, and anyway, my nan doesn't like sleeping. When she sleeps, she sees my grandad at the top of the road in his army coat waving at her. She tells him she's only going to be a minute, because she's just put a wash on. When she turns round, he's got fed up waiting and gone. 'Why doesn't he just come down the road and help you peg out?' I said. Nan said it doesn't work like that. 'It's just a nice dream,' she said. So I drew my nan winning the house on my card. 'Mum,' I said, 'is a hundred pounds a big win?' Mum told me to hurry up and colour my nan in. 'Make her skin pink,' she said. 'Her skin's pink, not white.' I told her that my pink felt-tip had dried up. Mum opened up her purse and started to cry. 'Write something soppy,' she said, 'just in case.'

Mum asked me if I had a fiver for bus fare and grapes. I said, 'Nan doesn't like grapes. They make her go.' Mum said that was the point. I said, 'But Nan's got a broken arm like Margaret Thatcher,' but I gave Mum my fiver because I'm not mean like my nan says Margaret Thatcher is. Nan says that Margaret Thatcher was so mean that she gave all her money to the rich people to make more money, and left the poor people with hardly any money to buy shopping. My nan can't stand meanness. 'You don't spend life from a purse,' said my nan. 'If that woman was still in power I swear we'd have oxygen tanks on our backs feeding it coins like a jukebox for the air that we breathe.' I said, 'Oxygen keeps you alive, doesn't it?' Nan said, 'No, family keeps you alive.' I'm dead glad my nan's my family. I'd be proper thick if it was just me and Mum.

Mum has gone to the hospital and told me that if I hear any noises or if a man comes to the door and I can spy on him through the bedroom net, I'm to call the policeman. She said, 'Don't use the oven, boil the kettle, or use a knife, and keep the telly on. That keeps away the burglars.' That was a treat. I'm not allowed to have the telly on after five o'clock. Mum says it's bad for my eyes and will make me go berserk.

On the news it said that Margaret Thatcher was doing well. I'm doing well at school. I wonder what Margaret Thatcher is doing so well at in hospital. I bet my nan's giving her a right earful. She's got lots to say about Margaret Thatcher. 'One day,' my nan said, 'I'll give that woman what for. She's made grown men cry.' It's not very nice to do well at making people cry. Those people are called bullies. Nan says that bullies are just jealous people and actually want to love you. Maybe my nan is bullying Margaret Thatcher and drinking all her Lucozade. Maybe Margaret Thatcher is still bullying my nan even when she knows my nan's bones are broken. I hope my nan has better pillows and more Get Well cards. I don't want my nan to be best friends with Margaret Thatcher. That would be weird. Margaret Thatcher would say our house was too small and needed a good bottom clean. She might even send my mum to war.

My nan said that Margaret Thatcher made us go to war but didn't have the bottle to go there herself. She just sent other people. She gave them guns and a ship and off they went. She said young lives got lost. 'Your grandad shovelled up his best mate into a wheelbarrow in the trenches,' my nan told me for my school history project. 'And when he came home, he used to drag me out of bed like I was a big gun he was loading. It used to make him cry.' I hope Margaret Thatcher's arm takes ages to get mended. Then she won't be able to write all those letters to all the presidents in the world about how many bombs they have and if they'd like to buy some more.

My nan once wrote to Mr Del Monte to tell him that she found a pear in her tin of peaches. They sent her a voucher for a new tin of peaches but she wouldn't spend it. She said, 'A pear don't make a peach.' My nan says that 50p to her might be nothing to others, but 50p is 50p and when you spend it on peaches, you expect peaches. 'I could've spent it on pears,' she said. 'But I didn't. I wanted peaches.' I went to the phone and called my mum. I said, 'Don't get grapes, get peaches. Nan likes peaches. They'll make her better.' I hope Margaret Thatcher doesn't have a bowl of peaches on her hospital cabinet. That will really nark my nan. Mum said it was too late. I checked the time. The shops had shut ages ago.

My nan has never left the country. My grandad went to Rome and freed some Roman babies. Then he came back and said the world was a dirty place. Nan said that Margaret Thatcher wanted to be American. 'She made us Little America,' said my nan. 'And when this country gets too full of people it will tip into the ocean.' Nan says we'll be OK though and I'm a good swimmer. I'll put my nan on a lilo and we'll sail off to Hawaii. They have dolphins there. People get mended when they swim with dolphins. I drew my nan another card. This one said 'Welcome Home Nan', and I drew her in her armchair with a whisky and the telephone and me. They're her favourite things. She said she needed no more than that. 'Margaret Thatcher won't beat me,' she said. 'I know what I'm meant for.'

Mum came home an hour ago and is sitting in the dark shaking, as if her body is a big bag full of broken bones all looking to fit back in their proper places. Sometimes bones just don't mend she said. Sometimes bones get buried or get burnt in pies, which is fine because kidney is rank and sticks to the roof of your mouth. Nan says some things should never go in your mouth and some things should never come out. Nan says we don't think about each other any more. We think only about ourselves. She said Margaret Thatcher taught her that. 'Call me old-fashioned,' she said. 'But values cost nothing.' I said, 'You're not old, Nan, you're thirty-three.' Nan said, 'Thirty-three dirty knees. I beg to no one.'

My mum was on the settee staring at the fireplace. I asked her how Nan's bones were. 'Sometimes,' she said, 'we're a pear in a tin of peaches. No one quite knows what to do about us.' I don't think my nan's bones got mended, so I rolled up the hearthrug just in case. Mum said, 'What are you doing?' I said, 'I don't want you to get broken.' Then I went to the bin and fished out that china sausage dog and washed it with Fairy Liquid like my nan would've done. It took me ages to glue on its legs and when I'd finished I put it on the hearth. Mum said, 'You'll make a good vet.' I said, 'No, I'm going to be like Nan and work on a pot bank.' Then I went into the kitchen and stuck a picture of my nan above the teapot. She'll like it there. That teapot's a Wedgwood.

Oceans of Stories

258 PEOPLE USED to live in this road and I knew everyone's names. I'd lie in bed, young back then, and count. Numbers 1 to 60 Ocean Road. The ten Arkwrights to Winifred Waters. 258 people, 258 names, not a single ocean nearby. No one saw the sea. Never thought the world would go faster and shrink the time we had in it because then they began to disappear.

I only ever saw them as people alive. Sweeping the front step, smearing Windolene on the windows while they washed their nets in bleach, those Arkwright kids sucking rhubarb stalks while they made motorways in the gutter. Back then, those days never slogged like hearses on motorways, barges on locks. We made stuff up when life wasn't exciting enough. We built new lands. We went there in gravy boats. But we always had a reason to come back.

258 people, 258 names. No one sweeps the front step any more. Like a multiplex this road with everything on show.

You can see what they've got but you can't call them by name. Children, you wonder—where have all those rhubarb children in gravy boats gone? 258 people, 258 stories. I could tell you many as now I can tell you none. We used to write stories with rhubarb stalks while our mothers swept the front step, boiled the nets, and wept at the kitchen sink.

We had a war and numbers 33 and 53 were lost at sea. That was their story. They went to sea to see what lived beyond the street, liked it so much they never came back. That's what mother said. Winifred Waters said they did it for us.

Our closest ocean was the bathtub. When our mother didn't cry, we made boats for the kitchen sink. 'Where's your boat going?' she'd ask.

'Not where those men went,' I'd say. 'Our ocean's got sides.'

'Don't listen to Winifred Waters,' mother warned. 'She's always been a wet weekend.'

258 people, 258 names. They forget I know their stories. We all paddled in the same ocean. Just because the road's changed doesn't mean I've stopped remembering. The last of the 258 we are. Him gone from next door, her over there gone snooty: we all had boats that sunk in the kitchen sink. Never occurred to me I should jump over the side, jump ship. I like sides. Wouldn't like to be seasick, and numbers 33 and 53 jumped over the side. Wouldn't do it for us now. The ocean's full of lonely old fish looking for a mate or to be hooked up for dinner.

A great tidal wave should come down our road. That'd startle them. Let the ocean do its cleaning of the front steps, nets and gutters, because 258 people once, 258 stories, and no one would come out of their front door and save me. No one wants to hear my story. Winifred Waters would. She'd say, 'All motorways lead to the sea, duck. That's where they've gone and they're not coming back.'

Dirty Laundry

You've been reading about the cuts and Icelandic banks but you only put two and two together when you're given your cards and see the state of your pension. You go and see Beattie—a steamroller of social action—who tells you to sit and stop shaking. You are fifty-eight, she reminds you, and not cheap.

'Alma,' she says, putting on bifocals to read your statement, 'you're lucky you even got that.'

She makes you a cup of a tea and lets you weep on her settee.

A week passes.

You're awarded a spray of tropical stalks to thank you for your forty-three years of service in the Town Laundry. There is no porcelain figurine, though you've dusted the hearth ready, and not everyone's found the time to sign your card. Your manager, Colin Nicholson, for whom you've developed a soft spot, sees you out with an awkward back-patting that reminds you of how Clive pets next door's Jack Russell before starting to sneeze for the rest of the day. He wishes you luck and calls you a stalwart, but you don't give a monkey's for being one of those. He smiles—like a hammock between palms on a tropical beach is that smile—and tells you again that retirement is all about you. Go be you. Do things for you. Enjoy being you.

You look at the pavement and say, 'But that takes bravery, Colin. And I am not brave.'

You carry home two trays of food in a flimsy carrier bag along with the tropical stalks that keep nicking your skin. You then declare to your dumbstruck husband checking his watch that one of the things you're going to do now you've retired is eat foreign food.

Clive tells you to try the new Asda and eats his rice with a knife and fork.

You, he calls you. What are *you* going to do?

You both take indigestion tablets before bed.

You dream of white bath towels billowing on the line like the old nappies, a grandchild burbling in a pram that has your eyes.

You have it all clear in your head. You'll take a room a day, the kitchen will take two days as the pantry alone is a day's work, and you'll start at the top and work your way down, room by room, inch by inch, until you're satisfied that each room can do without you. Then you rub in a little rouge and put on jewellery—a clasp bracelet with dim amethysts, a drop pendant your mother wore to church, wear shoes that give you a blister. Asda is further away than you thought but you must watch the pennies now, and you've not yet a bus pass. You ask at customer services when there's no one else around. The lad looks barely out of school and his shirt needs an iron. He asks for a CV. You tell him you don't have one. You've worked in the Town Laundry from fifteen years old until Friday. He says, 'Tills are full of women just like you.' But you don't look at the tills because you're thinking of what Clive will need and you head for the trolleys: stack up on cleaning products and have to take a taxi home.

You wear your best apron and rip open a packet of yellow dusters with your teeth. That's when it catches your eye: you're not wearing your wedding ring and you don't know where your wedding ring is. You do remember the day you accepted it. August 30th 1973. Clive Bunny's just told your father his first lie: he loves you and wants to protect you. Then he drops to his knees and sings as much as he can remember of Roy Orbison's 'Oh, Pretty Woman', which was, to your father's tuneless mind, wholly unnecessary when you're hardly a lass enjoying stacks of offers.

Because you're one of two daughters bookending a much wanted son whose heart pumped anti-clockwise and then stopped. You're the younger: a plain and daily Jane with a bowl-shaped face and a squint never corrected, and not long after your brother died you obliged Clive Bunny under army blankets: partly out of curiosity, mostly because your sister told you to—*Clive Bunny is as good a catch as you'll get.* You'd felt filthy after. Bathed until the water gave you a chill. You said no more until you were married: the dress pink, the darts unpicked, you'd felt blessed and soiled in one go.

You and him and her.

A year straggled past. Then two. The phone rings. A woman called June who suspects you're the wife. You tell her not to call again. You're decent people, working folk and besides, you've a little girl. She says, 'So have we, duck,' and slams down the phone. To this day you've never asked Clive if she's his.

You think about the wedding band Colin Nicholson is never without.

Some girls get all the luck.

You wear an old washing frock and set about your poky little bathroom with its avocado suite and postwar cherry tiles. There are fifteen toilet rolls stashed to the side of the cabinet, four towels on the radiator, six bars of soap under the sink, and your wedding photograph, hung on the back of the bathroom door to remind Clive who you are. You're also still waiting for a microwave, still hankering after a dishwasher, still hoping that your daughter will one day buy you an oven big enough to roast a 20lb turkey crown.

The weeping overcomes you. You sit down on the toilet and wonder what you're crying about. You realise it's the towels: the way Clive crams them onto the radiator after his shower so they stay all damp in the middle. You'll see these things all the time now. You'll know when he goes out and when he comes in, when it is he changes his underwear for you wash up to fifteen pairs each week. You cry for another ten minutes then pull yourself together. You go downstairs and fry liver and onions for Clive's tea.

You and him. And this is how it is.

You are cleaning your daughter's bedroom. A 4ft square with an ill-fitting blind and terracotta walls that give the room a dirty glow. If you get down on all fours, which Clive once asked you to do, you see, in the right hand corner, Julia's height chart: faded pencil lines showing her growth spurts from eighteen months until you forgot all about it once she'd turned four. You wonder how tall she is now. If she dyes her hair pillar-box red like she always wanted to do. You know she lives in Manchester where she went to study law. You know that she's a divorce lawyer, a partner in a firm, quite rich is what you hear, and that she hasn't set foot in this bedroom since Christmas 1992: the argument like yesterday, the things said still raw. You clean the room so furiously it gives you sores. Then you go through the usual motions, return it to the state in which she had left it: unmade bed, cocked-up blind, stone-cold mugs of tea idling on the desk, jaded posters of Debra Winger curled up at the sides. You've never understood your daughter's life, Clive even less so, and yet you lie back on her bed and take the phone out of your pocket to call her, like you do, once a week, letting the phone ring until the answer machine clicks in and you're forced to tell the ether it's *just Mum*.

You go downstairs and defrost the fridge.

It's cold in Iceland, you think. Life is frigid.

Clive is up early. Thursdays are a work day for Clive. Though he's nudging seventy, he's still part of a gang of ageing trackmen who tend to a particular stretch of railway where old and broken and vandalised trains are sent to convalesce. He's not paid to do this. It's just somewhere to go. And after the incident, or the accident, or the moment, as Clive calls it, when life, for whomever he was, could no longer be lived; after he'd watched it happen, right in front of him, near enough to call out to him, as he did, most nights, the nightmare living on, he'd been cajoled by an old doctor friend who'd thought a little tinkering about the tracks would do him good. And so he sups his tea early at the bedroom window and tells you, 'It's gone dark over Bill's mother's, Alma. I'd get your washing done this morning if I were you. Cats and dogs out there by four.'

You pad obediently to the laundry basket, begin to sort colours from whites, socks from pants, his from hers. You find them just after you hear the back door click shut: a crotchless pair of red rubber pants emblazoned with the words 'come in' which could be ripped on and off with a not-very-sticky Velcro.

It's never been just you and him.

There's a friend. Sort of. Pauline Roper. She pops in with news and brandishing photographs. Her daughter is pregnant again. Her other daughter's just delivered her fifth. *Nine grand-children, Alma. It's a ruddy good job I've retired*, and you chew the fat like two old dears on a coach trip, spending a penny together at a service station and passing toilet roll under the door. Pauline asks you, 'What you doing with yourself now you've got all this time on your hands?'

You look down at your hands.

'Look at my hands, Alma.' It's your mother's voice, pert and squeaky clean. 'My hands have been ruined by work, but at least they kept us out of the poorhouse.'

Yes mother. I'd be nothing without your hands.

Your mother had taken in other people's laundry when your father had failed to turn up his wages. 'A creased man is no man,' your mother would say. 'And his wife the last thing on his mind.'

It gives you an idea.

You've never suspected Pauline Roper but today, you do.

As Pauline talks you through the photos you think of your own. Many moons ago, you'd your own gallery lining the stairs. You've long put them from your mind, as there were many you threw away, and you think about what you have left, bubble-wrapped under the bed. You wonder when you stopped taking photographs, then wonder if you still own a camera. Perhaps you threw it out after Julia left, fearing there'd be no more stories to tell.

You realise that Pauline is telling you everyone else's stories: never any of her own as that would be telling. And then—*THUNK!*

You both rush upstairs to find a landing full of tumbled books and a warped set of shelves. Books that'd got Julia through her A levels—Maths, German, Law—what you'd paid for by squirrelling away money in an old tea caddy you'd kept quiet from Clive who distrusts banks as much as he distrusts saving when every day in his world is rainy. You and Pauline start to stack the books. That's when you find them. Not many, just some, and stuck to the pages of old and heavy law books.

The pictures are only mildly erotic, the women, despite the positions, often very pretty, and, though you're not entirely disgusted by them, Pauline reminds you that you must never forget what a clever daughter you'd brought into the world.

After Pauline leaves, you put the red rubber crotchless underpants on the kitchen table. You spend a long time staring down at the rubber circle with the words 'come in' printed sideways, then spend even longer ripping it on and off until its not-very-sticky Velcro completely loses its stick.

You think about the women. If any of them are still alive. You go into the lounge and shift the furniture around. Clean up old age and make room for grandchildren that'll never come—*I'm not dirty, Mum,* is what Julia had said. *And neither are you.* She had one suitcase at her feet. A rucksack on her back. You'd switched on the Hoover so you couldn't hear any more. By the time you switched it off she had gone.

But your house was clean as a pin. It *was clean* and everything put away.

You've been retired a week and have decided to go into business. *Beat them Creases.* You'll take in other people's ironing. You'll put postcards up in the newsagent's, maybe pop some through certain letterboxes up and down the street. You soap and scrub the hallway tiles as you think it all through then prise open the small hatch under the stairs which Clive had nailed up after you'd found that mouse. You use pliers and pull out the nails one by one. They are shiny nails. New nails. You prise the hatch aside and there it still is.

Clive's suitcase.

As you and Clive sit down for your tea, you think about the contents of the suitcase and how some genes aren't meant to be mixed. There was only a few days' worth of clothes in there. A train timetable. His mother's wristwatch stopped at half past four. Clive had never been able to pack properly if he'd ever packed a suitcase before, so you've repacked it with a few extras because you don't want people talking or for Clive to think that you hadn't looked after him right until the very end. Then after you'd repacked the suitcase, you'd got out your sewing kit and set about replacing the Velcro on those red rubber crotchless pants with four little black press-studs sewn on so tight that it'd test the patience of anyone who desired to ever *come in* again. You'd then put them in the suitcase and put it back where you'd found it, even hammered in the nails.

The weekend is long. You go to the chemist and buy painkillers, good ones, indigestion tablets, olive oil and cotton buds. You ask the chemist for an ear syringe. She asks if it's for you and you lie and say yes because your world is not falling apart. She shows you how to use it but you're not really watching. You're looking at how many different condoms the chemist sells.

You go to the newsagent's to cancel your evening paper. The newsagent says *not you as well*, and blames the paper-girl. It's not the paper-girl. You just don't like reading all that bad news every day. As you leave, you see your postcard in the window:

Dirty Laundry

Beat them Creases.
Let Alma Bunny Reduce Your Wrinkles for a Tenner!

You ask, 'Has anyone noticed my ad?'

The newsagent tells you it's only been up five minutes. 'But you can do mine if you like,' she says.

She takes you upstairs. You didn't know the newsagent had a life above the shop. You follow her into a kitchen with yellow walls and she asks you to wait. You hear an ironing board clanking. She shouts at someone, *where've you left the iron?* A teenage girl dumps an iron on the table for you. Neither of you speak. The girl's hair is pillar-box red and her eyelids are scuffed with black. The newsagent arrives with a basket heaving with clothes. She plugs in the iron and says, 'Tenner, right?' You have to agree because that's what you said, though you know Clive will scold you for not charging by the weight.

You iron for three hours with a view from the kitchen window. You're not offered a cup of tea and the iron leaks. You iron a uniform that is the same as Julia's was. Burgundy pleats. White shirt and burgundy V-neck. You remember how Julia would lose her tie. How you'd buy her another only for her to lose it again. You remember ink on the shirt cuffs. Blood once. Her jumper stretched by yanking—*someone's yanked this*, you'd said. *Like you've been in a fight.* You can see the look on her face. *You have no idea what it's like being me.* She was tall enough for Goal Shooter. Clever enough for a scholarship. And yet the teachers called her quiet. You'd frown and say, 'She never shuts up at home'—which wasn't true. She'd asked for a lock on her door at sixteen. You'd refused. You liked doors ajar. You used to sit in the kitchen below and think how quiet she was with her friend upstairs in her room. You'd go up with mugs of tea and no small talk. You'd find them the next day idling on the desk stone cold.

Homework. Studious. Debra Winger on her walls: the teachers had called her quiet, which she was. That was all.

You go back downstairs to tell the newsagent that you've finished. She goes up to check before she comes back to hand you a tenner from the till. But she doesn't get round to thanking you because she's got a customer who wants a lucky dip.

You go home. Clive is out. You do something silly: you swig from the sherry bottle and call Pauline. She's not in either. You could put two and two together but Pauline will have nine grandchildren soon and because you've had a sherry you tell her answer-machine that isn't fair.

Homework. Studious. Debra Winger. She was just quiet, that was all.

You check if the suitcase is still there. You count the times when you've packed a suitcase and wondered where to take it. You wonder what you've done with your wedding ring. You go upstairs to sort out your own laundry but you can't be bothered. When Clive comes home he finds you dismantling the deep-fat fryer. You tell him, 'Homemade chips. You can't beat homemade chips,' and you carry on: sorting through the parts, cleaning this, dusting that, wondering why it all won't go back together and fit into place until eventually, you tip the whole lot into a bin-bag and leave it on the street for the rag and bone.

You buy biscuits. The celebration sort. Belgian chocolate. It's like you've never been away. It's takes less than five minutes for you to don your tabard and help out the temp who's struggling with the jet-spray on the industrial iron. Colin appears. He's a lenient sort who carries no weight and he shouts you a vending-machine cup of tea. He thanks you for the biscuits, but next time you'll need to sign in and wait at reception. 'Had there been a fire no one would've known you were here to be saved,' he says.

'Wouldn't you have saved me?' And that is your voice, Alma. *Your* voice.

'Alma,' he says. 'You shouldn't even be here.'

It comes out of the blue. 'Please, Colin. Just a few hours. You don't understand.'

He looks down on you like he can barely see you. 'Alma,' he says. 'Give it a few weeks and we'll be the last thing on your mind.'

He smiles. You blush.

'Alma,' he says. 'You're wearing your slippers.'

You look down and then flee. You don't remember how you get to your street but once home you throw those tropical stalks in the bin because they're a pathetic bunch. Past salvaging.

There's a woman at your door. She has a wicker basket and is talking into a mobile. You don't recognise her but she's seen your ad. 'Any chance you can do this by five?'

You nod then she's gone; still talking to whomever it is on her phone.

The basket is crammed with clothes. You count twenty-three shirts. You need coat hangers. Because once ironed, those shirts cannot go back into that thin basket. You realise you haven't thought this through. Tools of the trade. Props of the professional: so you remove your own clothes from their coat hangers and most of Clive's because there were forty-six shirts in the end. They'd cleverly put one inside the other.

Pauline Roper comes round dragging a large basket and asks if you do mate's rates.

'I can't tell you how many people I've told about you,' she says. She clocks the other baskets in your kitchen that have replied to your ad. 'Well some of us are doing alright,' she sneers.

You tell her this one is on you. For old times' sake.

You go to the newsagent with a new postcard. You need to replace the last one, you say, because some of the details are wrong. The newsagent looks at the card and smirks.

'Putting your prices up already?' she asks. 'You're getting ahead of yourself.'

You put the new postcards in the bin on the way home and find someone has left a washing basket on your doorstep with a note: *from number 9*. Nine grandchildren, and you don't know anyone at number 9 when you live at 133. There's no phone number either. Instead, they call you. At 9 p.m. Clive answers. He doesn't know anything about ironing and puts down the phone. He says, 'Ruddy sales, at this time of night,' and you still don't know why you've not told Clive about your business: that you know there's a second daughter, and that you know. *You know.* So you tell him for the first time, 'I know.' But he's either not listening or he can't hear a thing because what he says in reply is, 'I thought we was ex-directory. You should call BT and complain.'

The basket from number 9 is full of baby clothes. You keep one of the baby-gros and put it in your knicker drawer because you like how it looks so pure. As you go back downstairs, you pass your own laundry basket which is very full. You've not washed your own clothes for almost a fortnight but you're a businesswoman now and you are busy. Busy, busy. And here is someone else at your door.

No one from number 9 has come to collect the clothes. You worry about the baby, there's a nip in the air, so you go and knock. It's Pauline Roper's pregnant daughter and she's not long moved in. She can't pay you either because her dole doesn't come through till Monday. You tell her she can owe you till then, it's fine. 'For the baby,' you say.

She says, 'Thanks,' and 'Always knew your Julia was a dyke. Don't that explain a lot?'

You rip open your knuckles on the way home by dragging them against the walls. Then you pack away all Julia's books into cardboard boxes and leave them on the street with the bins.

You are covered in plasters and smell of antiseptic. You think about those postcards with the new price and wonder what made you throw them away.

Homework. Studious. Debra Winger. Just quiet.

Some of us are doing alright.

You also told the bin-men to leave that cardboard box of books because it wasn't meant to be there. Hang around long enough, you joke, and my husband would throw me out too.

Clive's got a headache and not going into work. You tell him he has to. You've four ironing baskets to get through which you've stashed in the coal shed and you don't want them going damp. 'But I'm none too good, Alma,' he says, and wants toast, tea and a pill.

You go downstairs and have an idea. You crumble up one, then another for good luck, because last time you used them they didn't touch the sides. You put the ground-up sleeping pills in Clive's tea then take up his breakfast with the newspaper. You tell him to get some rest. You'll be as quiet as a mouse downstairs. Then you pat him on the leg.

It's practically a bear hug in your world.

Clive sleeps all day. This is no bad thing because the quietness is what you've been after. At 8 p.m. you check Clive's pulse. You convince yourself that everything's OK and set about syringing his ears because he's either stopped listening or gone deaf. There's another knock at the door.

You spend the rest of the evening ironing for whomever they are because, as seems to be the way, no one ever tells you their name or wishes to pass the time of day. At 10 p.m. a taxi honks. You use Clive's best belt to strap the basket into the taxi because you don't want all those lovely dresses spilling onto the floor. You ask the taxi driver where the dresses are going.

'Manchester,' he says.

You are sick in the street.

You run inside and check the side effects of the pills and wonder if it's an allergic reaction. Or maybe you've put Clive in a coma. In a panic, you dial two nines but put down the phone before the third. You root through the medicine tub again because maybe you've mixed up the pills and ground up something else. That's when you find your wedding ring. It must've slipped off your finger and dropped into the medicine tub one day as you rifled about for a cure.

But you have to call someone. So you call Julia. And when the answer-machine clicks in you tell her everything. That you've been retired and got these stupid modern flowers and not everyone had signed your card. That some banking hot-shot invested your pension in Iceland so you're ironing. Like your mother. So much you can't think. 'Because *you*,' you say. 'You and the women don't matter. It's *me* that's the problem. It's me.'

You remember Clive and run back upstairs. You find him on the landing rooting in the laundry basket. You mutter *thank God* and, 'What are you looking for, Clive?'

'Alma,' he says solemnly, as if he's about to come clean.

But no. He's counting underpants. He's no underwear left in his drawer. 'You've not been yourself awhile,' he says, putting the lid back on the basket. 'But this'—barely looking at you—'is bloody silly.'

You take the stairs two at a time, stand in the hallway and shout for Clive. As he comes towards you, you're surprised at how well he looks, how handsome all of a sudden, how lithe his legs, but because it's about time you started being brave, you kick at the hatch under the stairs until the panel comes loose. 'You've clean underpants in there!' you shout. 'Underpants you can bloody wipe down!' And you snatch the phone up from the hallway table and hand it to Clive. 'Ring her,' you instruct. 'If you can make your woman wear a pair of those rubber things you can accept your daughter for who she is.'

Now he looks at you. 'Woman?' he repeats. 'Christ, Alma. Is that what you think?'

What you think is what you thought you knew for a very long time and you could put two and two together and make the frigid wife to a cold-hearted man wired not to mind. But you don't. Instead, you watch Clive reach for the phone. 'No,' you say. 'We'll take the train to her.'

He looks alarmed and then starts to weep. 'Yes,' he agrees. 'It's time we took the train.'

You both take indigestion tablets before bed.

Happenstance

TEQUILA?

Why not?

Another?

No. Thank you. I'm done.

Come on. It's a celebration. I want to celebrate. Let me celebrate with you.

Why me?

You're the only person here.

You could celebrate alone.

I could celebrate with you.

What you celebrating?

Life.

Your life?

Your life, my life, all these lives with nowhere to go.

That's what you're celebrating? Dead-end lives?

All lives reach a dead end.

It depends upon what you believe.

I believe that all lives reach a dead end.

And you want to drink to that?

No. I want to drink to life.

With a dead end.

Then we'll drink to something without end if you'd prefer. We'll drink to love.

No. I'm too drunk to drink to love.

Why would you not want to drink to love?

Because I'm drinking alone.

You're drinking with me.

I'm drinking at this bar. You're stood behind it.

Then I'll come the other side and sit with you. Then you're not drinking alone.

But who will serve me?

I'll bring the bottle with me.

You're allowed to do that?

It's my bar.

Your bar?

You don't believe me?

How old are you?

How old are *you*?

It's just that, I don't know, at your age, I wasn't this, well, sorted in life.

You think because I own a bar I have a sorted life?

You're a lot more together than I was.

You only think that because you're drunk.

I think it because I'm old. Because my past's happened all too quickly. Because I'd like some parts of it back.

And what parts would you like?

I don't know. The good parts.

Like what?

That's none of your business.

Then they can't be that good.

That's not true.

Then tell me.

No.

No?

No.

Why?

Because they're *my* good parts. They belong to me.

But you only wish for those good parts, right?

I wish for my naivety. My strength. For all those lies I used to believe in.

And all those lies are what you want back? They're the good parts?

What is this?

I just wanted someone to have a drink with me.

Because you're celebrating your dead-end life?

No. Because this is what life's about.

Drinking?

Not drinking alone is a start.

There is more to life than drinking.

And yet we're drinking away our lives.

OK. I'll drink to something else with you but not for love. I never drink to love.

Because love's let you down.

Because love drives you mad.

Then let's drink to madness.

Madness?

Yes, madness. Madness that you should be drinking alone. Madness that you won't drink to love.

Madness is love.

Life is madness.

I'll drink to that.

And now we'll drink to love.

No. I will not drink to love.

Come on. Life is mad and short and filled with love. Drink to that.

No. You'll have to drink this one alone. I should go home.

Now you're making *me* drink alone.

No one is drinking alone because you will close this bar and I am going home.

Then drink this one with me to tomorrow.

What about tomorrow?

We're already in it.

No. Tomorrow is tomorrow. Now is today.

And you're certain about that?

I'm certain that you're mad.

One more won't hurt. We can drink to whatever you'd like to drink to. What about the good parts?

I don't want another.

I thought you wanted your good parts back?

But not in another drink.

You haven't moved an inch though.

I'm about to. I'm just finding my legs.

Legs that'll carry you home to who?

Me. I carry myself home to *me*.

And that's why you won't drink to love?

It's why I won't drink until tomorrow.

Then drink this one to hope.

We're drinking to hope now?

Yes, hope.

Hope for what?

Hope that there'll be somebody else to worry about you tomorrow.

There you go again. Making me drink to love.

I didn't even say the word.

You suggested it.

I don't think so.

You said that you hoped to be worrying about me tomorrow.

Me?

Yes, me. *No, you.*

You *are* drunk.

And that's why I won't drink to love.

Because there is no love?

No.

And no hope of love?

No.

And no tomorrow?

Well that depends.

Upon what?

Whether I can see it, whether it comes.

Doesn't it always?

Not always. Sometimes it passes you by and makes you wish you'd done it today.

Done what today?

Lived. Loved. Drunk.

Not hoped?

I hope every day.

You hope every day?

Don't we all?

What do you hope for?

I don't know. The stuff we all hope for. Love, life, tomorrow to be better than yesterday.

So you'll drink to hope but not for love and yet you're drunk because of all the hopes love never brought you?

That's not what I said.

But it's true.

I thought we were celebrating.

We are.

You've still not told me what we're celebrating.

I've told you. Life.

But what about life?

You won't drink to that.

So you are celebrating love?

I'm celebrating the hope of meeting the love of my life again tomorrow.

The love of your life again?

Yes.

And who is that?

You.

Me?

Yes.

What are you on about? You don't even know me.

Yes I do.

No you don't. We've only just met.

And you don't want another drink to celebrate that?

No.

But what are the chances of us meeting like this?

We could've met at the bus stop.

But we didn't. We met here. And we both hoped for it.

I didn't. I just wanted a drink.

But ask yourself why you wanted a drink.

I just wanted a drink.

And yet now you don't.

Don't what?

Want a drink.

I don't want another drink.

Because you're drunk or because you don't want another drink with me?

Both.

Both?

Yes, both.

So we'll have one for the road then and just say goodbye.

No. Really.

Come on. One for the road.

And where does the road go?

Nowhere. It's a dead end.

And that's the road you want me to take with you?

It's one road we can take. Or we can take another. That's up to you.

Why is everything up to me?

Because you want to drink alone.

That doesn't mean I want to go down the road on my own.

So it is about love.

No. It's about one for the *right* road.

One for the *right* road then. And then I'll go.

You'll go?

Yes.

But you own this bar.

I know.

So you can't go.

I can. I can leave you the bar.

But I need to go home.

You don't want the bar?

You want me to have the bar?

Yes. If you want it. It's all yours.

You're giving me the bar?

I need someone to have it. Why not you?

You're giving me the bar?

Yes. If you'd like it. You can have it.

I think I will have another drink.

Because now you're celebrating, right?

No. Because I need a drink.

Because what you hoped for you got?

I didn't hope for a bar.

You hoped for love though.

I never said that.

You hoped something would happen to change your dead-end life.

I never said that either.

So take the bar.

I don't want the bar.

It's yours. It's free. Take it.

I don't want the bar. I don't know how to run a bar.

It's easy. That's the good part.

But your bar is empty.

My bar is empty because there are other bars to choose from.

So you're giving me an empty bar?

Yes.

And you think that's a good thing to give the love of your life?

I think an empty bar is better than a full bar.

You sure about that?

Well you get to start from scratch. Fill the bar with what you want.

You're giving me this bar.

Yes.

Just like that? You're giving me the bar.

You don't believe me?

No. Not really.

Is that why you wouldn't drink to love?

What?

Love. You wouldn't drink to it because you don't believe in it.

That's not true.

So drink with me now to love.

We're going round in circles here.

And yet you thought you had a dead-end life.
No. That's not true.
Then drink with me to love. Or you can go home to *me*.
What about the bar?
You want the bar now?
You said you were giving me the bar.
Only if you needed it.
Needed it?
Yes. If you need it, if it will give you hope, you can have it.
You think I need your bar?
I can't answer that.
Why not?
Because I don't know you.
A moment ago you said I was the love of your life.
I said I hoped you were.
You hope I am?
Yes.
You're sure about that?
Yes. Aren't you?
No. No. I don't know you.
And yet a moment ago you'd have taken my bar.
You offered it to me.
And I'm still offering it now.
But you come with the bar, right?
I could.
I knew it.
Or you could just have the bar. That's up to you. You need
to make up your mind.
Can I think about it?
Only until tomorrow.
I might need more time than that.
Do you wear a watch?
No.

Then how much time will you know has passed by thinking about it?

I need to think about it.

What's the problem?

What's the problem? You're offering me a bar!

I'm offering you hope. A life. Another good part.

Oh, we're back here again, are we? Next you'll be asking me to drink to love.

No. I think I'm done.

You're done?

Yes.

But this is my bar.

So?

I'd like you to stay and have a drink with me.

I see. What will we drink to?

That's up to you. Tequila?

Why not?

Another?

No. Thank you.

Come on. It's a celebration. I want to celebrate. Let me celebrate with you.

The Cherry Tree

'THERE'S A WINDOW with cherries,' Roxanne was telling Thea. 'You've got two, three days at most before the birds have them. They'll clear a tree in minutes. So if it's OK, we'd like to pick our cherries right now.'

The cherry tree was at the far end of Thea's garden. It was part-way into summer and the weather was warm. Roxanne was standing on Thea's doorstep with her son, Toby, who had already announced to Thea that he was eight. This had made Thea look at Roxanne and then back at Toby. There must've been but fifteen years between them, if that, as it seemed that Roxanne was now pregnant with her second child. Toby was also carrying an empty shoebox which Thea thought very presumptuous.

'You see, the tree is rooted in *our* garden,' said Roxanne. 'But most of the fruit grows on the branches that are in *your* garden. We can only reach them if we pick them by standing on the wall in your yard.'

Thea did not like all this talk of yours and mine. Neither did she wish for Roxanne to come into her house which she would have to do to get to the tree. So she said, 'I'm sorry,' and closed the door.

The door, which Thea had recently repainted with a white emulsion, had two panels of frosted glass which she often cleaned with vinegar, so she was quite able to see Roxanne and her son still standing on her doorstep. She had also fitted an alarm and removed the doorbell.

'The cherries are mine!' Toby shouted. And in case Thea hadn't heard, 'They're mine!' very loud.

He then kicked the door and Thea scowled. Not only would this leave a scuff, but boys like this were a nuisance. Boys like that should be told.

'Ours, Toby,' Thea heard Roxanne cajole rather than scold. 'The cherries are ours. Be a good boy now. We must try and share.'

'Then tell that old biddy to share,' he said. 'Those cherries are mine!'

Thea could see Roxanne bending down to talk to her son. She had seen her do this once before in the corner shop. There, she had bent down and asked him, once again, to put the sweets down. They were not his. She didn't have enough pennies. And there were plenty of sweets at home. 'But I want these sweets!' he had wailed.

Roxanne had put a hand on his shoulder. 'No, Toby. The sweets belong to the lady on the till. See? She wants her sweets back, don't you?'

The lady on the till, and her name was Barbara, had smiled and played along: told the little boy that the shop didn't sell sweets after four o'clock. She was sorry, but that was the law. Then she'd turned to Thea, looked into her basket, and said, 'Is that everything?' which is what she said every week to Thea when putting her loaf, vinegar, rice and bleach through the till. Meanwhile, Toby had put the sweets into his pocket and left the shop.

What had happened next was strange. Roxanne, neither embarrassed nor alarmed, simply sidled out with two loaves of bread and a decent Chardonnay and never came back to pay for any of it.

'She's just stolen from the shop!' Thea had declared. 'Aren't you going to go after her?'

Barbara had shrugged. 'We know where she lives,' she told Thea. 'And it's just sweets,' as if that was all the explanation needed.

But it wasn't just sweets and Thea had felt confronted. That boy was naughty, she had said. He was wanting and he took without asking. That was stealing. He should've been scolded, shown right from wrong, and Thea decided that if she saw them again she would say this. Like mother like son, she would say. It's in his blood. And that he owed fifty-five pence for the sweets.

So that's what she said to the door that now stood between them. 'You never paid for the sweets, wine and bread,' she said. 'You stole from the shop.'

Outside, Roxanne said something to Toby that Thea couldn't quite hear. Whatever it was, it was certainly not what Toby wanted to hear, for he kicked the door again and harder than before. That would mean a second scuff. Possibly a boot mark. So Thea said it louder: 'I said, you never paid for your goods in the shop the other day. You owe for the sweets, wine and bread.'

Roxanne bent down and flipped up the letterbox. 'We'll pick them quick, I promise,' she told Thea. 'You won't even know we're there. Just let my son pick his cherries and that'll be the end of it.'

'I'm sorry,' Thea replied. 'But until you pay your way please go away. Life isn't about getting all your own way and your son needs to be shown there's a better way.'

'But they are *our* cherries. Legally speaking, we own the tree.'

Thea moved away from the door at this. It was true that the roots of the tree were not in her garden but the main boughs of the tree were. And though the tree required those roots to bear this fruit, Roxanne would have to walk through her house to get to that fruit. To walk through Thea's house was to know, and Thea didn't want anyone to know, as someone who didn't know (since Thea was not in the business of letting people in) would walk through her house and assume things: she's poor, they might think. She's mad. Or perhaps she has lost everything. Maybe given it away.

Thea turned away from the door and walked through her house. It was a long and narrow mid-terrace with rooms one on top of the other. From the hallway was the sitting room, which led into the kitchen and ended with large patio doors that opened out into the small garden where the boughs of the cherry tree took up more room than they should. She had, when she had first taken on the house, thought about chopping those boughs down. They seemed so imposing, allowing nothing else in the garden to grow. But the whole world was her family now. The whole earth was her home. She was clothed by the sun. And the cherry tree would live on.

Yet the roots of that tree had also spread under her patio. The paving slabs were lifting here, here and here. She had tripped often, the last time stubbing her toe so badly it had needed a stitch. So Thea went back to the front door and told Roxanne, 'You might own the tree, but I own the sweets,' and she pulled across the curtain she had fixed up at the front door and went back outside to look at the tree.

The tree, at this time of year, was glorious. The cherries were ripe. The leaves lush. Look up high and you could see just how many cherries this tree gave. It was impossible to count them. There was more than enough, though they were up high and ladders would be needed which she didn't have. But they were in her garden. That much was true. And then, the boughs seemed to suddenly bow to her, gifting her with their fruit. The cherries were within her reach. 'So if anyone will pick these cherries it will be me,' she said, looking up at the sky, and she went into the kitchen to look for a suitable container.

By now, Roxanne was hammering at the front door with her fists. 'Open this door!' she yelled. 'Those cherries are mine! Do you hear? Mine!' while her son kicked the door as hard as he could. And then Thea heard another voice: 'Is everything OK? Has something happened? Do you need to use a phone?'

Roxanne took no time in explaining her problem. She had come to pick her cherries from her tree but *this woman in this house* wouldn't let them. 'Those cherries are mine,' she told whoever. 'The tree is in my garden so legally they are mine.'

The neighbour, or perhaps just a passer-by, had now approached the door and was cupping her hands about her eyes and peering into the frosted glass. Thea overheard: 'I don't really know her. She's not one for mixing and there seems to be a curtain. Is she definitely in?'

'She's in,' shouted Roxanne. 'She told my son that he couldn't pick his cherries then slammed the door in his face!'

The neighbour appeared to be leaving, for she said, 'I can't help you I'm afraid. I don't know the woman and I really don't understand the situation. I'm so sorry.'

But Toby, used to getting his own way, was screaming. He would scream then kick the door, scream then kick the door.

Thea counted him doing this no less than ten times before Roxanne told him to calm down. 'Call the police!' he told his mother, and Thea suddenly felt so very afraid.

She leant against the hall wall. This was why she had never wanted children, why she had always wanted children, what she had done when she couldn't have children. She remembered the rage like yesterday, the kicks and the screams, the kicks and the screams. How her husband, her dear, patient husband, had covered his face with his hands: It's no one's fault, Thea. Not mine, not yours, it just is. Thea had detached herself from everything then, else she would have dropped out from life itself.

She looked up at the door again and saw that the wires from the alarm she'd fitted had come loose and were swaying in the draught like boughs on a tree.

The doorbell took her by surprise. Thea had thought she had disabled it when fitting the alarm. She looked up at the box on the wall and wondered whether she had, in fact, rewired the doorbell rather than wired in the alarm. Yet when the doorbell was pushed again it sounded brand new. She pulled the curtain slightly to see through the panels of frosted glass. A luminous yellow and law-enforcing black figure loomed. It pushed the doorbell again. Again, it sounded full of life. There was knocking. A polite request. 'May we come in?' Another knock. 'Might you open the door?'

Thea pulled the curtain right back and saw the three figures through the frosted glass. Had they actually called the police? Or had they simply been patrolling by? Thea moved closer to the glass and asked: 'Why are you here?'

'I'd rather you open the door, Madam, to speak with you,' and it was a thick accent that suggested somewhere north and perhaps to the west rather than the east. 'I am sure that everything can be worked out.'

The figure of authority, Thea could see, was of stocky build. They might need only to lurch a shoulder to ram the door open and Thea wondered who, legally speaking, would then have to pay for the new door. So she said, 'I'd appreciate it if everyone would go away.'

'Well, that can happen as soon as you open the door,' came the reply.

Thea thought about turning the key. Then she thought better of it. She must stand her ground. So she said, 'You do know that these people are criminals? They stole from the corner shop. I was there. I saw them do it.'

'Well, if you could just open the door now we can all sit down and have a conversation. I understand that this is about some cherries in a tree?' and it suddenly sounded so very silly.

'It's gone beyond the cherries,' Thea replied. 'Those people are thieves.'

'No one is stealing from you, I can assure you that. But please open the door.'

The three figures were now huddled together against the glass and Thea felt trapped. She was about to say, 'You are trapping me in my own home,' but another voice was speaking, a familiar voice, though one Thea had not heard in very a long time: 'What's happened? Is Thea alright? Is she in there? I have a key.' And Thea closed her eyes and sighed.

Fay.

'What's going on, Thea?' Fay enquired, pushing her key into the outside lock. 'Why won't you open the door, dear? Are you ill?'

This made Thea feel very guilty. She was not ill, that was just something else people would assume, and she tried to remember when she had given Fay a key. Then *why* she had given Fay a key. She tried to remember Fay's face—horsey yet pinched. How she would wear that certain look as Thea talked—serious and knowing. The agreeing nods. The disagreeing *hmmms*. And though Fay had been a friend, in the sense that she was someone who had known Thea well and at a particular time when Thea had needed such a friend, it had never been a friendship.

Still, she had given Fay a key. 'You know you'll have to give me a key, don't you?' And though one might assume that Thea was in danger, *a* danger, or that these were simply dangerous parts in dangerous times, a key had still been given and Thea could not at all remember why.

It was quite a crowd that had gathered outside of Thea's front door by now. Thea would have no idea who any of them were or why they felt the need to stop and listen to Roxanne's version of events. Thea could hear her and realised that she must be standing on the small wall outside of her house, all but three bricks in height, as if preaching. At one point, she was sure she heard a heckling 'God be with you!' But Thea was distracted by Fay, persistent with her key, pushing, no, ramming her key into the lock to try and push Thea's key out from the other side. The police officer cupped her hands through the frosted glass and called Thea's name over and over. Someone was holding a finger down on the doorbell and the din ripped through Thea's insides. 'The cherries are mine!' screamed Toby. 'THEY ARE MINE!'

So Thea turned her key and opened the door.

She was thrown by the flashes of cameras on mobile phones, just how many people had congregated outside of her house as if this was, indeed, a spectacle to be seen, and she immediately tried to push the door shut. Not quite in time, for the picture that appeared in the local paper had her looking frightened and thin in the sackcloth she now rarely took off. She would, for a long time after, wish that she'd just let them pick those cherries instead of standing her ground. They had, after all, come to pick cherries, not to see how she lived, why she lived as she did, how she punished herself for not bearing fruit. How she'd made a deal with nature, *unkind nature,* to understand why it'd chosen to renounce her as it did. But that boy was a nuisance. He needed to be told. And he and his mother were thieves. 'We can't always have what we want,' is all that Thea would say.

The wires from the alarm had only grazed the boy, but it was enough to give him a shock and a paramedic called. And although Thea had been astonished by how, somehow in the commotion, the alarm had come away from the wall leaving four big holes where she had drilled, she was secretly pleased that she had wired the alarm in correctly. Thine, O Lord, is the greatness, and the power, Thea had thought to herself. And in thine hand is power and might.*

As it was, the cherries never did get picked. Roxanne was right. The birds do have them. They steal from one another's beaks, fight over them, drop them, squish them, ground them into the slabs and spit out the stones, and the mess that was left behind on Thea's patio was nothing but thoughtless greed. It took many trips to the corner shop for cleaning products to clean up. In fact, Thea was forced to use so much bleach it killed the tree.

---

* 1 Chronicles 29:11–12.

Johnny Dangerously

THERE WAS ALWAYS a lot of us, like we'd all been born together one after the other, and we'd all hang out in the backs.

The backs were just that: the backs of our houses. Where the dogs chased the cats and the cats scratched the dogs and Natalie Mulally first showed Boof Moffatt her front bottom. 1, 2, 3, so that's what it looks like. Where we skanked fags and ran for ice creams always ten pence short of a 99. Where we booted balls and argued the toss and made pacts about each other's backs—*I'll have yours if you've got mine but I won't have yours if your father's coming.* Where we'd sit on the wall watching Kobin Mulally's mam getting into Mr Wheeler's red Beetle then dive behind it because Johnny Dangerously was coming.

Because Johnny Dangerously.

71

He was our hero. Always had been.

Johnny Dangerously.

We'd made his name up and we loved it. We didn't know his real name. Didn't know the half of it. Johnny Dangerously was invincible.

To follow him up close so that you could almost touch his denim jacket was a high score. Me and Boof Moffatt dared each other to touch it when we saw it hanging on the cloakroom peg at school. If we pushed our thumbs right through the tear on the shoulder we scored an eight. Nobody ever got ten. To get a ten you had to do something no one wouldn't ever dare do. Like when Kobin asked him to change a quid. His mam wanted bread. The crusty stuff with the speckled seeds because Mr Wheeler was stopping for his tea. But this was before the bread. When Kobin needed to use the school phone to call his mam to bring his PE kit. Johnny Dangerously was hanging around the phone at the time. He never went to class.

He goes to cooking class. He always goes to cooking class.

As if, Mulally.

He made a cake. This big and meaty cake. I saw him do it.

Shurrup, Kobin, you square.

But Kobin was right. Johnny Dangerously only ever went to cooking class. Nobody knew why. Nobody dared ask. But Kobin asked—

Got change for a quid?

—and got ten points straight away. Except he didn't because none of us were there.

I did! I said it! I said it right to his face!

But Johnny Dangerously didn't have any money.

Johnny Dangerously never had any money. Boof Moffatt once went without pocket money for nearly two weeks so he could be just like Johnny Dangerously. But then his favourite footie fanzine came out and he couldn't live without it so he had to ask his mam for the money in the end. Boof doesn't get free school dinners either. Johnny Dangerously has one of those cork cards that bags free school dinners and bus fares. We'd watch him flash it at Bubbles the dinner-lady then leave it on his dinner tray as if he weren't bothered about who saw he was a skank.

I dare you to rob his card.

That was Boof. Always daring us, never daring himself.

We'd know who he was then.

We went quiet. We hadn't thought about that.

I like it the way it is.

Don't you want to know who he really is? Boof asks.

I thought about it.

No. Not really.

But I still get ten points.

That was Kobin. Reminding us of his bravery.

I get ten points, right? That puts me in the lead.

No. That puts you in a headlock, spanner-face, with a judo chop to the shins.

I'll tell me *maaam*, Boof Moffatt! That hurt!

Kobin always said that. No one took any notice of it. His mam was never at home for him to tell her anything. Kobin's sister Natalie was always sitting on their backyard wall with her skirt up her arse and swanking about how many times she'd let her new boyfriend Chigsey put his pigeon in: 47, 48... 73... a hundred!

My mam says your mam's a floozy!

Your mam's *the* floozy and I'll tell *my* mam about *your* mam!

Well, why's your mam always in cars with other mums' men?

I am. I'm telling me *maaam*!

And tell her your Natalie should start charging. My mam says she's bloody daft giving it away for free.

Duff. Duff. Duff.

Kobin's punches never connected.

Tell her yer effin self.

Kobin had been wearing the same school shirt for almost two weeks. It reeked like a dirty dishcloth. Only the gypsy-girl Annaleza wore the same school shirt for two weeks. Annaleza only had one shirt. Annaleza sneaked to school because her mam didn't want her to be too clever for a husband.

You share your shirt with Annaleza!

Shurrup, Boof! I'll tell me *maaaaammm*!

We could've carried on. Made Kobin cry and given him a dead leg. But Johnny Dangerously was coming. We forgot about Kobin's shirt. Kobin forgot to tell his mam.

He's got no fags.

It's not the same.

He's got no money. I told yer he's got no money.

That was Kobin. Still going on about his bravery. Boof kicked him in the shins. Then he took five points off Kobin's score for being boring. He'd never catch up with mine and Boof's scores now.

He's still brilliant. Whatever you say. He's still my hero.

Our hero.

That's what I said.

We'd got a game against Salley Grange so couldn't follow him. I scored twice and did my celebratory tumble. Scoring twice meant I'd have to get up on stage and shake Goldstraw's hand in Friday assembly. Everyone would clap and I'd get picked for five-a-side no sweat. Boof didn't score any. He blamed Kobin and gave him a mud sandwich. Boof hated losing and he hated not scoring. Then he took another five points off Kobin for not toughening up.

I got a quid for my first goal and fifty pence for my second. Mam play-punched my shoulder blades and said, 'Yer dad would've been ever so proud,' and then she locked herself in the bathroom for a very long time.

Kobin came to school again with the same shirt on. There was a mud stain all up his back. Goldstraw said, 'Kobin Mulally, my office now!' and everyone in the corridor stared.

He were there!

Who was?

Johnny Dangerously. I stood with him. Right up close.

No *waaaaayy*!

Are you shitting me, Mulally? Are you shitting me again?

Honest, Boof. He were there.

Boof had got Kobin in a python-lock with his thighs. I was emptying things out of his schoolbag; one for every wrong answer.

I swear on Blue Nan's grave, Boof!

Boof nodded at me. I crashed Kobin's pencil case on the ground. Everyone knew that Kobin's Blue Nan was an old tinker who was always after your gold. She used to read your tea leaves and knew all about marriages and all about death but never knew if you were going to be born a boy or a girl or if Stoke City would win the FA Cup. She didn't even know that she was going be run down by a bus or that we called her Blue Nan because of the big veins running up and down her legs.

Liars always get found out.

Boof nodded and I snapped Kobin's compass in half. It nicked my thumb and made me bleed.

He weren't in class and he's been ragging some kids for money, Goldstraw said.

Another nod and I chucked Kobin's dictionary down a manhole.

Honest, Boof. It's not a lie! Owwww!

Chinese burns and dead legs at the same time were Boof Moffatt's speciality.

Kobin had to see Goldstraw about the state of his shirt. Johnny Dangerously had been found smoking in the staff bogs again. They'd stood in Goldstraw's office together. Friday detention.

Where's your mother, Kobin? The work number I have for her is out of service.

Kobin had shrugged. He was too small to look Goldstraw in the eye.

Has she changed jobs, Kobin? What does she do?

She's a nurse.

Kobin always lied about his mam. She worked behind the bar down the Bingo where Mr Wheeler called out the numbers. Two fat ladies, eighty-eight. Maggie's den, number ten. Mr Wheeler gave her a lift home every night in his red Beetle and sometimes came in for his tea. Kobin's dad worked the oil rigs. He sent him letters with photos of the rig. He had a black face in the photographs. His arm around another man with a black face. They were smiling. Big white teeth and oily knuckles. We called Kobin's dad Captain Rig but no one had ever met him.

Will your mother be home this afternoon, Kobin? Can I call her then?

Another shrug.

She's saving people's lives.

Kobin hardly ever saw his mam. She came home in the red Beetle really late when Kobin was asleep. One night she didn't come home at all and Mrs Manfred from next door had to go into him because of all the crying he was doing. He said there was terrible moaning coming from the pantry. Mrs Manfred made him a hot milky drink and tucked him up tight. Mrs Manfred wore a wig.

And you're behind with your schoolwork again, Mulally. Does your mother not help with your homework?

Course she does.

Shrug. Pout.

That's what mams do.

Mrs Manfred stayed up with Kobin until his mam came home in the Beetle with Mr Wheeler. She did his homework then knitted him half a jumper while she sat and waited for the Beetle and his mam to come back. Kobin's mam never knew Kobin had a babysitter. Kobin's dad was on the oil rigs. He didn't know anything. Kobin's sister Natalie was out painting the town red with no knickers. My mam says that Mrs Manfred might not see Christmas.

Kobin had started blubbering. He blubbered a lot when ragged about his mam. Goldstraw didn't like blubbering kids in filthy school shirts. He liked smart kids and crisp shirts that smelt of starch.

Kobin Mulally, you'll pack in those tears before I pack them in for you.

And I'll pack you a few punches if you do because I'm a bit sick of men like you telling us how it is.

Because Johnny Dangerously.

It was Johnny Dangerously.

He'd stuck up for Kobin *and* was going to belt Goldstraw. Kobin's score doubled.

He did say it. I swear on Blue Nan's grave he said it.

My mam says all you Mulallys are bog breaths. She says you talk shit.

He did, Boof. Honest he did. I anna lied to yer once.

But Kobin got a dead leg. Then a cauliflower ear. Then Boof took all his score away for lying.

Not everyone's got a mam, you know.

That was Johnny Dangerously. He was telling Goldstraw how it is.

Some of us don't even get a dad who wants to know either.

You're a born liar, Mulally!

He did say it, Boof. That's exactly what Johnny Dangerously said.

What about your parents, Goldstraw? Did they stick around or did they leave you with the nuns cos they couldn't be arsed?

Honest, Boof! He told him how it is and it were brilliant! And then he put his arm round me and said he'd look after me.

Kobin looked at the ground.

He's still my hero. I don't care what you say.

Because Johnny Dangerously had walked Kobin home that night. Kobin's score shot through the roof. Johnny Dangerously had wanted to know what Kobin had that he hadn't and he took his computer, the microwave, and the fifty quid that was kept under the kitchen sink for emergencies.

What about my score, Boof? How many points do I get for Johnny Dangerously being in my house?

Boof Moffatt said scoring was for babies.

He was only lending it, Kobin moaned. He'll give it back. He promised me.

And that Johnny Dangerously didn't exist.

Later, Kobin said that Johnny Dangerously's knife was massive and gleaming and blood dripped off the end. Only Mrs Manfred said she believed him.

I never told Boof, but after Johnny Dangerously got expelled, I found his cork card that bagged him free school dinners and bus fares. It was just under the bench where he used to hang his denim jacket on the cloakroom peg. Back then, if we pushed our thumbs right through the tear on the shoulder we scored an eight. Nobody ever got ten. To get a ten you had to do something no one wouldn't ever dare do. Like when Boof Moffatt phoned the cops and grassed him up. Or when I flipped over that cork card and saw his name was Kane Wheeler. I chucked it in the canal on the way home and never told a soul.

Featherbed Lane

1.

THAT BREDA IS so mad alarms Frances. 'Why?' she keeps on shouting. 'Why won't you remember?'

'Because I don't,' Frances tells her again, and she covers her face with her hands and stops herself from remembering anything. She knows that underneath her hands is a small forgettable face that will give nothing away. That she has, over the years, practised this face like Breda used to practise piano (manically), went on to practise medicine (diligently), and she is good at it now, giving nothing away. She is the story that will not be told.

As for Breda, her face is big, round and frustrated. As she shouts you can count her fillings (six), catch sight of one enlarged tonsil (on the left), smell the rage on her breath. She hasn't changed much. Still tall. Almost pretty. Bit more weight. And glasses now. There'd not been glasses at school. Though the laugh is the same, throaty and forced, the sort of laugh that makes you glare. And the voice: coarse and scratchy as if she means to clear her throat. 'Come on, Frances,' she says again. 'You're not remembering on purpose.'

Frances thinks this is a childish thing to say. 'If I knew anything I'd have gone to the police.'

But Breda cannot hold back. 'You were found on the heath, Frances. It was happening right in front of you.'

'I still don't know what it is you think I won't remember.'

'But you do remember.' Breda smiles. 'You're remembering it all the time, Fran.'

Frances scoops up her daughter Clover from the floorboards where she's been poking between the grooves with a wooden school ruler. She takes a moment to breathe in her daughter's hair, to dust off the malted milk biscuit crumbs from her mouth, to remind herself just how lucky she is. She is calm now, clear, able to ask Breda once again for their coats. She would like to take her daughter home.

Frances will tell no one of what happened that afternoon. It is not kept like a secret. Rather, she cannot find the words to describe how it all came about. One minute they were sitting in Breda's kitchen drinking coffee, the next and Breda's mobile had begun to ring. She'd jumped up from the table, listened to the call for what, nine, ten seconds at most, then asked Frances if she would mind keeping an eye on Reuben because she had to go.

'You don't need to go upstairs to see him,' Breda had said, zipping up a leather jacket that looked and felt its price. 'He'll only panic if he knows I've gone out and I'll be half an hour at most.'

Breda did not tell Frances where she was going, but threw keys and a purse—was it a purse?—into a bag, a black leather clutch bag, saying, 'I mean it. Don't tell him I've gone. Stay downstairs. Help yourself to another coffee. There's plenty of stuff in the fridge for your daughter.' And then she'd added with a faint air of threat: 'I hope you understand.'

2.

They had not been friends at school. They knew each other, knew of each other, had socialised a handful of times on unremarkable occasions. Neither Breda nor Frances much remember those times. Breda has tried to but Frances has not.

After school came college. Frances had put both Breda and school from her mind. Breda had thought of Frances occasionally. Then she'd found herself thinking about her all the time. And yet Breda had not seemed to recognise Frances at first. Frances had not seen Breda at all. It was Breda who tapped Frances on the shoulder.

'Hello, *you*.' And then, 'It is *you*, isn't it?'

Breda had started talking immediately. She was married. Surrey boy. Rob? Rod? Met at a wedding somewhere down south. She was drunk. So was he. But she knew. She said he knew too. She wore an engagement ring the size of a grape.

She was a doctor. Dementia. Alzheimer's. Therapeutic work, she did explain, something about reconditioning damaged memories and how madness was but momentary: 'Because if the brain can forget how to breathe, it cannot be culpable for all it might've done.' But Frances had lost interest after hearing the word *doctor*. Breda was always going to be a doctor. Saving lives. Inventing cures. No. Her husband wasn't medical. He worked in construction. Sympathetic renovation. Had spent two years doing up their place on Featherbed Lane and was now working fourteen, fifteen-hour days to compensate, on a building site for Taylor Wimpey. 'He's got a lot to make up to his highness,' Breda said as Frances muttered under her breath, '*You live on Featherbed Lane?*'

His highness was their son, Reuben. Five years old and home-schooled. They'd been trying for another ever since, got a specialist on the case now, exploring IVF. She was forty-two next year. He'd be forty-eight. There's plenty of time, Breda had said. No age is old any more, and his highness is just dying for a little brother, though she would like a girl. 'You want things to be perfect, don't you?' telling all this to Frances in Sainsbury's car park where they'd met after twenty-six years. Then Breda had clicked her fingers in Frances's face. 'Remind me. God. It's so embarrassing not to remember your name.'

'Frances. My name is Frances.'

Before they'd left each other, Breda had asked for Frances's number. They must meet up, she'd insisted. 'Now that you're back home.'

Frances had been startled by this. 'I'm not back home.' She'd needed this to be clear. 'I'm just here, that's all, and not for long.'

'It's been longer than that, Fran,' and Breda had smiled. 'Don't you think that it's time you brought her round for a play date?' She'd peered into the buggy. 'Drop-dead. Got your eyes. What's of his?'

Frances had made something up. 'Hair. Flyaway. Quite thin.' Then, 'She's not yet two, Breda. She doesn't really play yet.'

Breda had waved this away. 'Twenty-six years!' She'd said it again.

'Yes,' Frances had agreed. 'I suppose it is.'

'So, who do you see then? You know, from school?'

Frances had thought this unkind. She'd dropped her head. 'I've lived away a long time, Breda.'

'Well, you know who's kicking around? Sarah Lalley. Gave up New York to come back here. Three kids now. Husband's from Detroit. We've had them to dinner twice. And Hannah Middleton. You remember Hannah Middleton? You sat next to her in History for two years. She's a chemist. Still hilarious. And Madeline Bishop? Come on, Fran! Madeline Bishop! Though I doubt she'd remember you.'

Frances had fixed her expression. 'School was different for me, Breda. The girls were unkind.'

'Only because of how you were.'

But Frances had been distracted by the contents of Breda's trolley. Ten, eleven—no, twelve boxes of Fruit Shoots, she'd counted. Six packs of Kinder Eggs, a surprise every time. Breda had followed her eyes.

'He doesn't really drink all those Fruit Shoots,' Breda had explained. 'I decant them. Replace them with tap water. I have to pretend a lot these days, don't you?' And then she'd gripped onto Frances's arm as if they really did know each other well. 'Twenty-six years,' she'd said again. 'Can you really believe it's been twenty-six years?'

Frances had looked down at Breda's hand on her arm. Long fingers. Splayed fingers. Piano-playing fingers. Another thing she was good at. Except she bit her nails now. But not all of them.

'Play date,' Breda had repeated, removing her hand. 'Then we can catch up properly. You're at your mum's, right? I'll call, because I've really got to shoot.' And then she'd just stood there as if she'd got something else she'd wanted to ask.

Frances was not stupid. She knew what Breda had wanted to ask. She could see it in her face even without looking at her. But then Breda had seemed to think better of it.

'Twenty-six years!' she'd said instead, as if she'd forgotten to say it before. And then she was gone. She drove a large black

Audi, black leather seats; it was as much as Frances knew about cars.

3.

Frances's mother, Jane, knocked on her bedroom door to ask if she was decent. The mug of tea appeared first—'With a splash of Dutch courage. Don't tell Derek. It's his Talisker'—her face all smiles, her hair cut too short these days and feathered into the back of her neck. Frances was sitting beside a pile of clothes, smarter clothes than the vest she had chosen to wear that would happily fit a small child. She was paper thin. Gaunt. Dark around the eyes. She'd wear no make-up. Often, her mother had to say, 'Rub a bit of rouge in, Fran. At least look like you've got self-esteem.'

But it was hard not to see the hurt still dulling Frances's eyes, to know that she'd not begun to mend. It was coming up to a year now and yet she'd made no progress. Still wept. Still yearned. Used drink to sleep. At the funeral, at the graveside, Jane had slipped her hand into her daughter's and said, 'No one can stop a train crash when it's already crashing, Fran. He knew what he was doing,' but Frances had been adamant: He didn't. But we did. And she'd let go of her mother's hand.

Now, sat by the pile of clothes on Frances's bed, Jane tried again. 'Talk to me, Frances,' she said. 'We all loved Timothy. Not just you.'

But there was that look again. The one that told Jane to back off. You didn't love Timothy like I loved Timothy because if you did you wouldn't have sent him away. So Jane asked where she was going.

'To see Breda,' Frances said.

'Do you need the car?'

'No. She lives on Featherbed Lane.' She paused. Should she tell her mother where Breda really lived? She decided not to.

'And you're happy to go there?' her mother asked.

'It's where she lives.'

'Even so.' And there was concern in Jane's eyes. 'Couldn't you just go into town instead? Meet in a café?'

'They're just houses, Mum.'

'Houses on *Featherbed Lane*.'

'Don't do this. Not now.'

'Well how many kids does she have?'

'One. He's five.'

'That's manageable in a café.'

'Stop it!'

Jane picked at the threads of a blanket on the bed.

It is a single bed. It is the back bedroom. The curtains are the same and so are the walls. Jane has not got round to redecorating, and though she is ashamed by this, Frances is happy that the room is as she left it twenty-four years ago. Jane did mention to her husband that it might be nice if her daughter could come home to a different wallpaper, at least give the idea of a fresh start, but her husband has other things on his plate and doesn't altogether agree with this decision that his wife and step-daughter have come to. He thinks Frances should buck up her ideas and remember she's a mother now. Children take priority. She had a job. She should get another one. She's qualified, isn't she? She went to university. But Jane thinks otherwise. She should've helped her get her own place. Put a bit aside. Saved. 'She needs a home of her own,' Jane had told Derek. 'Somewhere that has no memories of here.'

Because a year or two after Frances's father had walked out, a girl was found dead which started all that trouble down Featherbed Lane. 'They were brutal with her,' Jane had explained. 'She was just a child. She'd not seen a thing.'

But Derek ignores the bit about the murdered girl and the disappearing dad and thinks about the awful lot that has been, he believes, of her own accord. He's yet to be convinced that Frances has cut all ties with Clover's father for instance—he is sure he saw her with a mobile phone only the other day—as he fears that her coming home will interfere with his and Jane's retirement plans. He has seen his wife with Clover. She's already mentioned that quitting England might not be an option just yet.

Jane looked through the pile of clothes next to her. 'What about this?' she offered her daughter. 'I've always liked you in this.' And then, 'Goodness, Fran! How old is this? You must've had this since you were fourteen.'

Frances looked at what her mother held up. A navy-blue V-neck dotted with purple pearls. She'd remembered the last time she'd worn it. No coat. Barefoot. Running up and down the street. Where was everyone? Why didn't they answer their doors? Maggie, in the ground-floor flat opposite, finally opening her window to her: 'I've called the police, Frances. Someone has to do something for him.' *But where did he go, Maggie?* Which way did he go?

Frances pushed the thoughts and the V-neck aside. It reeked of the heath. Of the dust and the dog shit and the butts she used to collect for Timothy who'd split them with his penknife and tip the hairs of tobacco onto a white saucer—always a white saucer—until he'd enough to roll up. Then she'd watch him smoke, see the relief on his face. Oh, that was good, Frances. *That was good.* And she'd smile, never really understanding what her big brother had just rolled up. He was here. He was back. And that was all a little sister ever wanted.

Shh! He would grin. *Don't tell a soul.*

Frances picked up yesterday's denim shirt and started to put it on.

'This friend,' Jane asked. 'What did you say her name was again?'

'Breda. Her name is Breda.'

'Wasn't she the one who did that performance, you know, about the…' There was a long pause. 'The one that made all those accusations? About what happened?'

Frances was debating between scarves. 'Yes. That was Breda.'

'And you're still going?'

'It was a long time ago.'

'What she did was disgusting.'

'It was only a play.'

'It was grotesque. Threatening. You didn't sleep a wink for months.'

'It was her way of dealing with it.'

'And what about you, Fran? Have you dealt with it?'

Frances had knelt to the bedroom floor to look for shoes.

Black linen pumps. She'd been wearing these delicate little black linen pumps. He'd asked her to take one and leave it on the lane so other people would see and know where to look. 'Because I haven't done it,' he'd told Frances. 'She was already here.'

Frances had opened her eyes as wide as she could. She'd almost seen his face this time, the colour of his eyes.

'I'm going to be late,' she told her mother quickly, and busied herself with the toggles on Clover's winter coat.

4.

Breda's house was a livid-looking gloomy red brick with a bathroom on every floor, a hallway long enough to roller-skate up and down and a kitchen table that'd comfortably seat a conference. When Frances had lived here, as a child, she'd had two rooms to herself: a bedroom she'd slept in and a den she'd played in, though in there she'd lived the most, under the eaves and between the floors where her parents fought about what she can never remember.

It'd been an inheritance. An old spinster aunt of Frances's father's who'd been persuaded not to will the whole place to her cats: ten of them, abandoned at her death, spayed quickly then put up for sale with a sign at the bottom of the road. They'd arrived with three suitcases—there was no need for furniture, the house was full of it—and though there was no mortgage, it was a house for many more than they were. The house quickly buckled under their tiny little routines. They barely touched its sides. Her father was, at the time, an architect on a junior's wage who dreamt of skyscrapers, buildings so tall they looked down on the rest of the world. Her mother worked in Thornton's to pass the time. Paid in pennies and lots of toffee that got stuck in your teeth. Then, one day, her father never came home at all.

The house had to be sold. There was no question of that. Frances and her mother took on a two-up-two-down facing the park until they couldn't afford that either. Her mother was adamant. She didn't want any fuss but didn't care who knew. So she invited people in. Everything was for sale. Frances remembered: walking the shops into town, she saw their television and stereo in Eddard's Electricals, her bedroom furniture up for grabs in Furniture World on the corner of Melloncroft Drive. She'd just turned fourteen, options and mocks pending, so her mother went to see the headmistress of her school to make some arrangements. *Not special treatment. Just some understanding. She's feeling left behind.*

Derek seemed to come out of nowhere. He lived on the council estate that skirted the heath, all but a cock-stride from Featherbed Lane, their old home just visible from her bedroom window if Frances stood on her tippy-toes. Tin town, as it used to be known, the houses built after the war to sustain another war, and not long after they'd moved in, Timothy had come home too.

Breda closed the door behind Frances. The click of the lock made her flinch. Breda noticed. 'People sell houses. People buy them,' she said to Fran. 'It's not that weird being here, surely?'

Frances watched Breda change into a pair of black pumps, the sort they used to wear for P.E. They made her look grief-stricken and Frances remembered that look. For a long time it was all that Breda wore.

'What do they call you then?' Breda bent down to address Frances's daughter.

'Clover. Her name is Clover.'

'Where did you get a name like that from?' But that was as far as Breda's interest went. 'Reuben, they're here! Switch it off!'

Frances had forgotten about the son. There were protests over a television being switched off. His voice was choirboy high. He stumbled into the hallway with two grazed knees and a grey sweatshirt that claimed he was a Dude. 'Reuben, this is Clover,' Breda introduced the children. 'She's come for a play date. I expect she'll like your Duplo.'

'Hi, Reuben. How are you?' Frances spoke for her daughter.

'Fine.'

He was a pretty little thing with big eyebrows and didn't look like he was used to having friends around.

'Reuben. Take Clover to your room.'

Clover had clung onto Frances's shin.

'Go on. Go upstairs with Reuben. He has toys up there.' Breda pointed towards the stairs.

'She does this when we're somewhere new,' Frances began to explain. 'Teeth. You must remember. It goes on for months.'

'She's just got no siblings,' Breda snapped. 'She wouldn't be clinging onto you like that if she was one of many. What happens if you just leave her?'

'I'm not going to leave her. She's never been here before.'

'That's ridiculous, Fran, you lived here. She's feeding off your nerves.' Breda bent down to address Clover at her level again. 'Reuben had to learn that Mummy couldn't be with him always, didn't you?' She beckoned her boy closer. 'Go on Clover. Go with Reuben. He has toys.'

'Breda, please. She's just a baby.'

Breda told Reuben to go to his room anyway.

Frances spent a long time looking around Breda's kitchen, perhaps longer than she thought. At the muted colours: flax, straw. At the solid oak table, the price of a second-hand car. The church pews used for dining chairs. The sharp corners and marble surfaces. The heavy bone china displayed on dressers. The wine. A noticeboard. A calendar. A wedding invitation for June. There was a recipe for something French. Her name was on the calendar. *Frances 3 p.m.* But no Reuben. No pictures. No paintings. No child's mess. No fingerprints on the window. No chocolate smudges on the wall. Frances had wondered: who cleans, who cooks, how much was their mortgage? And why here? This house on Featherbed Lane. Where the willows really did weep into the stream that flowed at the bottom of the garden. Where the road bent and buckled into its dead end, beyond it the woody heath with its hawthorns and heathers, its dust, dirt and dog shit, and the death that would never go away. Where Frances had been sent to collect fag butts for her brother who was broke but clean—*I'm clean, Fran, squeaky clean*—which she'd watch him split with his penknife, tipping the hairs of tobacco onto a white saucer—always a white saucer—until he'd enough for a roll-up to smoke. Where the girl had been found, disturbed by badgers, a shoe on the lane, a naked arm bent awkwardly across her face as if she'd just fainted. Frances had been seen barefoot and running, not long before it'd happened and not far from where the girl was found, with her roller-skates in her hands: *But where did he go, Maggie? Which way did he go?*

'Cream and sugar?' Breda asked, handing Frances a large white mug of black coffee, and the thoughts stopped.

'You know, I saw Becca Oakley last week. Remember her?' Breda dumped a plate of malted milk biscuits on the kitchen table. 'Her marriage broke up last year. He was a pig by all accounts. Obsessive. Wouldn't let her out of the house hardly. Had to go and pick her up myself to get her to come for a coffee and she sat there, just like you, clockwatching and nervous and refusing to engage.'

'I'm not your patient, Breda.' The coffee in Frances's hand smelt burnt. 'And I've told you. I don't remember much about school.'

'You wouldn't be here if you didn't.' Breda sipped her coffee. 'Aren't you in the least bit curious about me?'

'We didn't all make Oxford.'

'Is that what you think?' and Breda looked Frances straight in the eye. 'Don't be fooled, Fran. This house, this life, it all comes with stipulation. And no, I didn't go to Oxford. I had a breakdown. Two, three years of my life, completely blank.'

Frances glared. 'I didn't know,' she began.

'Well, you weren't the only one, you know, if that's why you're here.' Breda poured more coffee. 'I was ringing people all the time, every night, saying the same thing. I'd lost my best friend. And she was, Fran. She was the love of my life. Someone knew something. You were just unlucky, I suppose.'

'But I didn't know anything. I didn't know her. Didn't even know she was missing.'

Breda started to smile.

'You always didn't and never did.'

Frances looked down into her coffee, chewed on her lips.

'You know, they say that the brain, being a muscle, can be trained like you'd train for a marathon,' Breda lectured. 'That actually we barely use it. That the brain sees far more than we'll ever be able to comprehend because we simply cannot entertain all that we see in every second of time and contain all that information to assure ourselves we've seen it and as it is. It's why we never really look at what's happening right in front of us. Can't see the wood, as they say, when you've been murdered in the trees.'

'She wasn't in the trees.'

'See?' and Breda clicked her fingers in Frances's face. 'You do remember.'

Except that's when Breda's mobile began to ring. She'd jumped up from the table, listened to the call for what, nine, ten seconds at most, then asked Frances if she would mind keeping an eye on Reuben because she had to go.

'You don't need to go upstairs to see him,' she'd said, zipping up a leather jacket that looked and felt its price. 'He'll only panic if he knows I've gone out and I'll be half an hour at most.'

Breda did not tell Frances where she was going, but threw keys, a purse—was it a purse?—into a black leather clutch bag. 'I mean it. Don't tell him I've gone. Stay downstairs. Help yourself to another coffee. There's plenty of stuff in the fridge for your daughter.' And then Breda had added with a faint air of threat: 'I hope you understand.'

5.

Frances did not go upstairs straight away. She'd only gone looking for Reuben when she'd realised that Breda had been gone for almost an hour and was worried he must be hungry. The first door she'd opened was obviously the boy's classroom.

A smallish brightly coloured party of a room with dangling planets, maps and buckets of toys with goldfish tanks set into the walls. No, Reuben told Frances later as she made him a sandwich. His goldfish didn't have any names. They couldn't remember them so there was no point. Had she never heard of a goldfish memory?

Later, when Frances can't sleep, she will close her eyes and dream of Reuben sat in his classroom at his little desk and chair, his pencil poised on a blank white sheet of paper that he starts to draw lines on very straight and going nowhere. So he takes another sheet of paper and continues the line, darker this time, straight down the middle of the page, and he carries on, a third piece of paper, a fourth, fifth and sixth, until Frances wakes up and realises she's got it wrong: only his mouth was black. The rest of his face was white. He was a white man with a black mouth.

Frances backed out of the classroom and closed the door, knelt down to Clover's level and said, 'Where's Reuben? Shall we try another door?'

They'd found him squat among beanbags, one hand clamped around a joystick, the other holding onto a purple Fruit Shoot while a TV, as big as the pool table set for a frame in the far corner, screened a computer game Frances didn't recognise. Out of the corner of her eye she saw the vending machine: Fruit Shoots and Kinder Eggs, a surprise every time. She was moving towards it to believe it when Reuben switched off the console and asked, 'What are you doing here?'

'What did you say?'

What are you doing here?

He was looking down on her and wearing glasses. Thick lenses, dark rims, she could barely see his eyes.

What are you doing here?

The rest of him was black. Coat, shoes, trousers, whatever was under the coat, probably black. It's why Frances had thought the whole of him black, including his face. He was holding a black shoe.

You're not supposed to be here.

Lager, stale lager, tobacco, threads of it about his lips, and that smell: the smell her mother used to dread that he'd try to disguise with aftershave sprayed all over his coat.

What are you doing out here? It's late.

Roller-skating.

One skate on. One skate off.

You shouldn't be out here. Not now. Something's happened and it wasn't me.

It had not been a man's voice but a voice pretending to be one.

And that's when their hands had somehow met. Except Frances was still holding onto her roller-skates—there'd been dog shit all over the wheels—and now he was holding onto her arm? Or her elbow? Her hair? He had grabbed her hair with long fingers. Piano-playing fingers. Nails that needed cutting for a man.

She's in my den. They put her in my den!

No. No.

I want to show you. I haven't done it. She was already here. Let me show you!

As there's always the possibility that Frances wasn't there at all.

It's my den and she's in it. We need to get her out. They'll think it's me.

Frances had screamed.

Come with me. Come and see!

She started to scream. She clamped both hands over her mouth.

Come with me!

What?

'Come with me.'

'I'm sorry... What did you say?'

'Come with me so I can show you my den. Come on. I want to show you what I've done in it,' and Reuben was tugging at her shirt.

Frances stumbled out of the room as if suddenly drunk and needing to throw up. Except Clover. Where was Clover?

'Reuben, where's Clover? Is she with you?'

'Nope.'

'She was here, Reuben. Where the hell did she go?'

'You said you would come and see my den.'

'What have you done with my little girl?' Frances stopped breathing. 'Clover. Where are you? Shout to Mummy. Clover!'

She pushed open a door and yelled her name. Pushed open a second and flicked on lights though they were not needed and shed on nothing, Reuben, all the time behind her, and telling her it was only a den. Just a den. There was no one in it. Pushed open a third.

'Clover. Thank God.'

Frances sank to the floor in a different room.

Later, when Frances thinks of this room, she will not remember the headlines and the stories and the notes; extensive notes made like a detective and chronologically arranged. She will not allow her mind to recall the photographs or the missing posters or the ones that replaced them asking for witnesses. She will only remember the one in the centre that was hard to avoid: of two girls half-smiling, five years between them yet their cheeks pushed together as if they'd been born hours apart. She will only remember the list of suspects, many of whom Frances had been to school with. Sarah Lalley. Hannah Middleton. Madeline Bishop. Her own name was at the top of the list and when she'd looked at it she'd smelt lager and aftershave and dog shit really strong. Eyes: she is sure that when she hit him with her roller-skate he got dog shit in his eyes because he didn't run after her though she'd kept on running. No coat. Barefoot. Running up and down Featherbed Lane. Where was everyone? Why didn't they answer their doors? Maggie, in the ground-floor flat opposite finally opening her window to her: 'I've called the police, Frances. Someone has to do something for him.' *But where did he go, Maggie? Which way did he go?*

By the time Frances had arrived home the tin house was in darkness and the phone was ringing. She'd picked it up because there was no one in the house to answer it.

She's dead, isn't she? They'll find her tonight and she'll be dead. Was it you? Did you do it with your skates? I bet you did and I'll tell.

The planting of a thought that became a memory of being accused—Frances had been the last person Breda had called—and she'd put down the phone and raced back to the heath because she should've brought her big brother home.

6.

Frances was coming down the stairs with her daughter in her arms when Breda returned, some two hours later, and long after Frances had found Reuben, in his den, and seen all of the rooms in the house on Featherbed Lane. Breda looked up at Frances on the stairs.

'What are you looking for, Frances? Something to remember?'

'Your son was hungry,' Frances snapped. 'You've been gone almost two hours.'

'He knows where to get refreshment when he's hungry.'

'That's a vending machine, Breda. Who has a fucking vending machine to feed their kid?'

And that's when Frances sees there's something different about her. She can't quite put her finger on what, but she definitely looks different from when she went out.

Except Breda is mad, and that she is this mad alarms Frances. 'Why?' she keeps on shouting. 'Why won't you remember?'

'Because I don't,' Frances tells her again, and she covers her face with her hands and stops herself from remembering anything.

'Come on Frances,' Breda says. 'You're not remembering on purpose.'

Frances thinks this is a childish thing to say. 'If I knew anything I'd have gone to the police,' she says.

But Breda cannot hold back. 'You were found on the heath, Frances,' she shouts. 'It was happening right in front of you.'

'I still don't know what it is you think I won't remember.'

'But you do remember. You're remembering it all the time, Fran.'

Now Breda offers Frances wine. It's red and it's cheap and it'll taste of sawdust, but her stomach is already turned and she needs to go home. She asks for their coats then scoops up her daughter Clover from the floorboards where she's been poking between the grooves with a wooden school ruler. She takes a moment to breathe in her daughter's hair, to dust off the malted milk biscuit crumbs from her mouth, to remind herself how lucky she is. She is calm now, clear, and she asks again, 'Our coats, Breda.' She would like to go home.

'You weren't the only one,' Breda tells her again. 'I was ringing people all the time, every night, saying the same thing. I'd lost my best friend. And she was, Fran. She was the love of my life. Someone knew something. You were just unlucky, I suppose.'

Frances looks down at the floorboards and hears the rolling thrum of her roller-skates as she goes up and down the hallway.

She hears her parents arguing one last time in the kitchen. The thud of her father's shoes as he storms out, never to come home again. She thinks briefly of the two-up two-down that lasted not a minute before her mother had shacked up with Derek; before the hospital called and her mother was forced to sit Derek down and tell him: 'I have a son. And he's not been very well.'

Not very well: Jane had had to explain. She went back a little: the teachers had called him agitated. She called him just busy. A doctor prescribed pills. She'd thrown them away. He turned thirteen. Restless. Bored. Neighbours got burgled. Friends got darker. He liked a girl who didn't like him. Liked another who broke his heart. He was seventeen when their father left, Jane had explained. And he was taking whatever he could get his hands on. So, I did what I had to do.

Frances turns to Breda. 'How did you know about the skates?'

'What?'

'When you called me on that night. You said, *did you do it with your skates?*'

Breda flushed. 'I don't remember saying that.'

'You did. You said, *did you do it with your skates?*'

'You were there, Frances. Not me. And you *do* remember.'

Frances took in a deep breath of the house. 'This house will tell you nothing about me,' she told Breda slowly. 'And she was already dead. Dead, they said, ever so long before he found her.'

Breda grabbed at Frances's arm. 'He?'

Frances looked down at Breda's hand on her arm. Long fingers, splayed fingers, piano-playing fingers. Except she bit her nails now. But not all of them.

'He died, Breda. My brother died. That's why I'm back here. So now it's just me who knows who was really there.'

Breda released her grip. 'Timothy?' Her face glowed. 'He's gone?'

Frances nuzzled into Clover's neck. 'He was in no position to take anyone's life when he could barely live his own,' she told Breda sadly. 'I didn't see that then, but you did. And my brother has saved your life,' and she and her daughter left their coats behind.

7.

January. Eight months later. Frances finds out via text message that Breda has had a baby boy. Everything is perfect anyway. She hopes Frances will bring Clover for a play date. Reuben would like that. So would she. We still need to reminisce, is what she texts. I'm thinking of organising a school reunion.

Frances will remember their last visit, how she'd thought Reuben looked nothing like his mother, that she'd not seen a photograph of Breda's husband to know if he took after him. She will also wonder how many others Breda had tracked down from school and lured into her house to see her room. Names on a list. Suspects in a crime: there was still no news about the dead girl and would not be for years to come. Not until Breda remembered herself. *Because if the brain can forget how to breathe, it cannot be culpable for all it might've done.* Until then, she would remain the girl found, disturbed by badgers, a shoe on the lane, a naked arm bent awkwardly across her face as if she'd just fainted, right there on the heath aside Featherbed Lane.

I haven't done it, Fran. She was already here.

When Frances thinks of him it's always with their father's shamed face. And then she sees him for who he really is, a boy who could not be, and wishes, with all her heart, she had just taken him home.

Frances will read Breda's text and delete it. Then she'll throw the phone out of the car window. She will watch, in the rear view mirror looking back along the road she has travelled, how it smashes into a thousand black plastic pieces, like ants in a line and trying to survive. And it will jog her memory: Breda had come back into the house wearing a completely different set of black clothes.

Smear Campaign

I KNOW I SOUND like an old chuff but that van of his was getting on my wick. It was blocking my daylight. I was having to put my desk lamp on by two o'clock and you can't be blaming the ozone for that. Dark blue navy transit it is with blacked-out windows and even the registration plate looks swindling. I was just thinking about calling the police when his mother finally came round to tell me what she'd done.

She's gone an old-fashioned bread pudding of a woman has Petal, and she's all trussed up in a mustard frock with a bunch of yellowing tulips clashing at her breasts. I hadn't seen her in a while and she'd had that pearly perm done again that washes her out. I've told her before about hairdressing on a shoestring.

'And I've told you about minding your own,' she snaps as I let her in, and she's whiffing already—nose in the air and eyes on the prowl—but there's no point either of us being peevish. All water under the bridge now, getting on for over thirty years. 'I won't beat about the bush, Arnold,' she says, taking off her gloves. 'But I've given our Joseph the house. He says he's ready to come home,' and then she adds, albeit under her breath, that his marriage has broken down.

I raise my eyebrows. I didn't know he was married.

'There's a lot I wish I didn't know about you either, Arnold Bunter,' she says. 'It still makes my stomach curdle to think about it.'

I roll my eyes at her. I knew she'd been in next door cleaning its hind legs off with disinfectant and anticipation for the best part of a fortnight, and though I had my suspicions I didn't get my hopes up.

'It's as we said, Petal,' I told her. 'But I'm still surprised he's coming home.' And I was. Very.

'Well, you leave him be till he's ready,' she goes. 'Remember I know you.'

'And I know you,' I said back, but we shook hands in the end and said thank you. Hearts are captured all over the place and never given back as they were.

'Oh and Wilf's wife's dead,' she said as if telling me she'd just scrubbed the loo. 'Thought it best you hear it from me,' and then she was off. Goes the other way these days, up the hill towards the old folks' new builds and looking down on everyone else, just as she wanted it. But we've promised each other clean graves so you could say we've moved on.

Still, after she'd gone I had myself a little cry. Not much, but enough to soak half a hankie.

Our Joe moved in next door quicker than I expected. Great big van turned up, three lads to help, two double beds. I'd got the front bedroom net hitched up with a couple of paperclips and had brought my big teapot down from the top of the dresser and given it a scalding—it gives four good mugs at a push does that pot—and I thought they might help me out with the last of the Christmas cake. I was spick and span otherwise, cock-a-hoop to be honest, had been ever so flamboyant with the emersion, I was taking a bath every day I was that excited, but that's me. Can't suck on a toffee log either. Guzzle down a whisky before the whole round's been poured.

I had it all set out on the tea tray for them by midday, four mugs of tea, four wedges of cake. They'd been working hard heaving in all that stuff. Two of the lads had taken their tops off. Bulky arms they'd got. Muscles on muscles. The type to squeeze you to death and make you feel safe as ruddy houses.

I made it down the hallway with the tea tray then bottled it. Can't so much as knock the skin off a rice pudding these days, it's been that long since I left the house. Still, you can't rush these things and it's a lot to ask of the lad so soon.

I thought me and our Joe would only see each other again in death. Dramatic, I know. But that's me. A bit of a crisis keeps you alive.

I left our Joe a Post-it on his wheelie bin as we trundled into March. By then, I knew where he'd hung every picture, where every appliance had been plugged in, smelt what he was having for his tea, but couldn't quite make out which bedroom he'd chosen to make his own.

'I warned you,' Petal shouts down the phone at me. 'What do you think you're playing at with them notes? Have you forgotten what's round your ankles and why it's there?' But her bark's worse than her bite.

I said, 'It's daft this, him being next door, me rattling about in here with nothing doing. It's been almost two months, Petal, and not a dickie bird.'

'Well, you're still dead to him,' she says spitefully.

I spot an eyelash on my teaspoon and change the subject. 'And what's that bloody van all about anyway?' I says. 'It's been almost two months.'

'It's his house now, Arnold,' she says. 'And it's as we all agreed. So if he wants to park a van he can park a bloody van.'

'Now look here Petal…' because I was on the last of my patience to be frank.

But that was a red rag to a bull if there ever was one, because she goes, 'No. You look here. It's because of your bloody looking we're all having to live like this. What about folk looking at me, Arnold? What about folk looking at him?'

I said, 'No one's looking at anyone other than themselves these days Petal. I've told you before, if you can't look inside…' but she'd slammed down the phone by then. Not that stuff like that smarts any more. Between you and me, it just bounces off the sides.

A couple of weeks pass and I'm just letting my dinner go down when Petal comes to see me wearing her sensible brown shoes. I said, 'I told you that bunion wouldn't thank you for those peep-toe heels.'

She says, 'You're hardly one to be lecturing me about bloody peeping.'

But that's the trouble with old wounds on old skin. The little blighters just won't heal.

She said, 'I want a word. Are you busy?'

I was having a slice of Madeira cake so thick with butter you could see my teeth marks. I didn't tell her that I'd been putting that Madeira cake out for over a week now, just in case our Joe popped in, dusting it with a drop of milk now and then to make it look like I'd just had it fresh out of the oven. I had my tricks as Petal had hers, but I could see she'd come to tittle-tattle so I put my hand on her shoulder and smiled. She pushed it off roughly and wiped herself down with her handkerchief.

'Oi,' I says, all offended. 'I'll have none of that when you're in my house. Clean as a pin, me. First time I've sat down all day, yet I haven't so much as heard a Hoover going next door. Makes you wonder what he's doing all day.'

'Working men, Arnold,' she starts up, 'go *out* to work all day,' and I can see she's trying to start something but I won't be reeled in.

'Well he's gone nowhere in that van,' I says, pointing at my calendar. 'It's been there sixty-five days now. That's surely a traffic conviction.'

'He's kitting it out, numbskull,' she snides. 'He's waiting for equipment.'

'What sort of equipment?'

And I can see she's itching to tell. She leans forward and beckons me in. 'It's best it comes from me,' she whispers. 'He's window cleaning.'

I can hardly get my breath.

'I know,' she says clocking my face. 'It winded me a bit an' all.'

Petal makes me sit down and pours me more tea. She spits in milk, adds sugar, two lumps, then asks if I've any brandy. I says, 'Should I just put a bucket on my head and give it a kick or what?'

She looks surprised. 'Buckets?' she says. 'Buckets!' as if I haven't heard. 'There's no buckets, Arnold. It's amazing. Totally sterile glass they call it. Spotless window cleaning and not a smear left behind. He showed me last week how it worked on the bungalow. Then he went round Margery's and asked if he could show her what it could do for her conservatory. I said, "What do you think, Margery? Isn't it amazing?" And our Joe says to Margery, "You'll have to let me give your Gerald a price for his office block." And when he sees her face he starts laughing. "See this pole, Margery?" he goes. "It's got no limits. Glass ceilings this, reach up and clean God's arse,"' and she finally took a breath. 'But you'll never guess what the best bit is?'

I shook my head at her. I'd no idea.

'Doesn't even need a ladder,' she sniffs. 'Privacy you see, Arnold. Professional privacy.'

'I see,' I stutter out. 'So what's next? Bloody skyscrapers?'

She smirks so hard it cracks her lipstick. 'You should ask him come do yours,' she says. 'Because you might've been a window cleaner once, Arnold Bunter, but you can't clean your own for bloody toffee.' And she struts out of my house and into the day as buoyant as you like.

I go and dream of our wedding day again that night. Wilf goes to me, 'I've forgotten the rings on purpose, lad.' And my hands are shaking and I'm fiddling with the lilacs in his buttonhole and that's when I whisper in his ear: 'I promise.' Because Wilf only came home from the war because of me. He'd been that terrified he'd actually lost his sight and then a fair bit of his mind. So, I made him the sort of promise that only exists between men who've seen war.

But then the trumpets start up and there's Petal, all on her own at the back of the church in her homemade frock and breaking her heart. I've never forgiven Petal for arriving like that. That sort of sympathy takes over your heart. When I turn about Wilf's gone. I shout his name but I've no voice and I'm rooted to the spot and the vicar puts his hand on my forehead like he's blessing me and goes, 'You know what you are son? The boy who cried Wilf.' I wake up soon after, sweating cobs I am. Pillow's drenched.

I was still mithering about that dream when I drew the front curtains the next morning; I almost missed it:

BUNTER'S WINDOWS
clean, transparent & smear-free

In big yellow capital letters it was, slapped across the side of that navy blue van. We had a ladder and a bucket in my day. Kind hearts who'd give you a cup of tea and a squirt of Fairy Liquid to sweeten you up for a bit of gossip about the new folk at number twelve who were either a pound short or never in when you wanted paying.

I sank into the armchair and wondered what to do. Though perhaps what I should do is put a few things straight:

Window cleaners aren't just window cleaners. They're neighbourhood watch. Age concern. We see everything. We know what you've got. And we've got a bit of time of day too. So if we see something we shouldn't or think you've not got what you thought you had, then that time of day is what we give the Old Bill. Solved many a crime have us window cleaners. I even caught a bloke with his pants down before his second stroke. He's ninety-nine now. Tells me if he gets a telegram from the Queen he's going shove it up my arse.

But I didn't choose to be a window cleaner. I was going be a plumber. After the National Service, of course. That was my father's trade. Plumbing. And drains. Was partial to a bit of guttering as well in the winter. Some men won't climb a ladder, you see, and leaves, when there's a lot of them, can stop a train in its tracks. No. It's was Wilf's old dear who gave me the idea. 'I'll never know what my husband sees in you, Arnold, but I see straight through you like a bloody dirty window,' she once said. I never liked the woman, she only ever saw everything for what it was, but I'm decent enough to thank her for that.

Of course, she's not the only one to think like she does. The quacks will tell you different. And the quack that was sent round after Wilf took his last breath had me housebound and tagged which, he says, is cheaper for society than being locked up. Though I've never owned a computer. You can think what you like, but I can promise you that I wouldn't even know how to switch one on.

I chose April Fool's Day to go round next door in the end.

'I know I promised but I need a word'—and how I got those words out I don't know for my hands were shaking like a hedgehog in a log-pile. 'Can I come in or you come in to mine? I've got some things I'd like to say.'

He's aged not so well close up, our Joe, bit too whiskered for my liking, hazelnut eyes, biscuit skin, the spit of his father back in the day, when I could still turn a few heads, and he's put a lot of weight on around his middle. He just stands there leaning against the doorframe and shoves his hands in his pockets. Defiant little bugger. He should've felt the back of my hand there and then.

'You really want to do this on the doorstep with all these nets twitching?' I says.

He thinks on. He weren't ever the cleverest stick in the bundle, hardly going to set the world alight, but he steps out of his house and shakes his shoulders as if he's limbering up for a box. Blimey, I think, as I back away. What's this to be? A punch-up in the street? And he's a much bigger man when he's stood outside the house, looks as heavyweight as a dead pig.

'Come on now, son,' I say. 'It's been thirty odd years. You and me need to leave this past behind.'

'No, you come on,' he snaps, and he goes to the van and unlocks its doors.

It doesn't take him long to get going. Starts on about all this newfangled window-cleaning equipment. This pipe here is what gets rids of all the impurities and this part here absorbs all the dirt from the air, while this filters the water, over and over, up to four times until this siphons off all that's contaminated: the stuff we want rid of and can never clean up. It was like looking at a chemistry set. 'Shame we couldn't have filtered you four times back then,' he chides. 'Might've kept my dad a man then.'

Now here's where I might have a bit of explaining to do. I'll start by saying that he wasn't well was Wilf. Cancer had got him by the throat. His wallet was in the back of his trousers on the bedroom chair and his Mrs had gone see her mother. So I went upstairs and sat on the bed, asked him if he needed owt fetching from the chemist or the ale shop and he pulls me towards him and says, 'You promised me, Arnold Bunter. You made me a promise in a house of God that you'd stop all of this.'

I said, 'I know, lad. But I've a disease with no cure too.'

He says, 'Then kick the bucket, Arnold. Like I am.' And he reminds me: 'We always said we'd go together.'

'That was in war, lad,' me now reminding him. 'We was seventeen then and shit bloody scared. And don't let us forget that if it wasn't for my pair of keen eyes, me and they wouldn't have made it this far.'

He pulled us in for a hug then. He well remembered that bit and I'd saved his life a good many times. So much so, he patted my back with the last of his strength.

But outside, our Joe had climbed up my ladder. Little nipper thought he was helping his old man out. Christ knows what he thinks he saw because he says to me that night, 'When it's my round, Dad, I'll be cleverer: have a bigger ladder than anyone. Then I can see everything that's going on, what everyone's up to, what everyone thinks they've got. Just like God.'

Never spoke a word to me after that. Told everyone what he thought he saw and never stopped. You'd hear this, you'd hear that: Petal believed it all, Joe wouldn't even look me in the eye, and that was that. No more cleaning windows.

'I'd rather have dirty bloody windows than be able to see what you really are, Arnold Bunter,' some said. But there were no open minds back then.

Then, as it happened, next door went and came up for sale. I thought to myself—if that's not God telling me to stay put then I don't know what is. I was able watch my lad grow up from the bedroom window. I couldn't ask for any more than that.

At least that's my version of it, but as Wilf's Mrs was always keen on reminding me: 'Remember Arnold, you can see through a window both ways.'

It was no use me trying to make sense of all this new equipment. I didn't really care what our Joe did and how he did it. I was just chuffed he was back. So I says, 'The thing is lad, what you think you saw that day, between me and Wilf, was a promise between men who've seen war.'

He comes towards me. So close I can smell the Fairy Liquid on him. 'I know what I saw,' he says. 'What sort of man you are *and* what you've seen since.'

'Son,' I says. 'What I like to see isn't what I like to do.'

But I could tell he was still convinced it was more than that. So I pointed at the hose system in the back of his van.

'Get this up and running then,' I says. 'Go on, son. Finally get it out of your system and see if it works.'

He never even asked if I was joking. He just started up that equipment, unleashed that hose and blasted me to kingdom come with God knows how many gallons of that purified water. But I'll tell you this for nothing. However hard that water came at me and knocked me down, four times filtered or not, I still got up on my own two feet and faced him.

I couldn't tell you for how long he did it. It was over thirty years' worth of pent-up rage and a fart of wind that'd blown Wilf's bedroom curtains aside for Joe to see what he thinks he saw. Like I told my son then as I tell him again now: 'I was a window cleaner for a reason, son. Better that than going down any of those other roads you can go down. But you carry on thinking what you like. Just come down from that ladder one day if you can. Be nice for me and you to have a pint.'

'But that's just it, Dad,' he says. 'I don't need a bloody ladder.'

And he turned his back on me, coiled up the hose, turned everything off, closed the van doors and walked back into his house.

Pick Up Your Socks

From the Bride to the Groom

WHEN I THINK ABOUT love, I am picking up your socks. This is not the only pair that I've found. They are here, on the stairs, and there behind the chair. There's a pair stuffed in your boots. I trace a smell to a purple pair, inside out, and there's a hole, in the sole, so I throw those ones away. I find a sock in the washing that has no other, and it's this one I think about. It must've been part of a pair: you or I will have bought a pair of socks to wear as a pair. So where did it go?

I emptied the sock drawer in case the odd sock was there. But there was no one sock. Just pairs. Twelve years of our socks, actually. Socks we wore here and took there. Black socks. Striped socks. Ankle socks and tights (those are mine, at least, I hope they are mine).

I realise that we wear each other's socks now. We no longer care for which are yours and which are mine. We share everything else. And now even our socks. My left to your right. My right is your left. But we no longer need those sorts of directions. Socks are always one and the same. And yours are more comfortable anyway.

Then a little voice asks for her socks—'A blue one,' she says. 'And an orange one. Just like Daddy.' And she's putting on a sock of yours over one of hers, though perhaps it's one of mine. No. It's one of ours, and it's definitely the one I thought we couldn't find. It's far too big for her, but we let her wear it, pulled right up above her knee. It makes us laugh. She laughs too.

'We're a three-sock family,' she says.

And I realise that's what odd socks are for. When a pair becomes three. None of this yours and mine. But our sock drawer.

The Land of Make Believe

YOU TRACE IT ALL back to £5 worth of Woolworth's vouchers you don't spend for a year.

You eventually get Bucks Fizz on cassette because *Look-in* gave it 10/10. You sing along with the wooden end of the skipping rope in front of the full-length mirror in your mum's bedroom. *Stars in your eyes. Little one. Where do you go to dream? To a place, we all know. The land of make believe.* You are Cheryl Baker. You only learn the words to her parts. You paint your nails the colour of a goldfish, just like Cheryl Baker. Oonagh Macnamara, who's as fat as her name, says it looks like you've been smoking. *Dirty fagger,* she says and gets everyone to chant—*Dirty fagger, dirty fagger*—and no one will sit next to you because you stink of fags. So you sit on a desk that juts out on a table for four like the fifth member. 'Everyone knows that the best groups are always a four,' says Oonagh. The Fab Four. Abba. Bucks Fizz. 'You're just the groupie,' she says. 'And everyone knows why they're with the band.' And those are her mother's words as you'll come to know that this is what girls do.

Mum says you can use her nail varnish remover but don't use all the cotton wool. Both cost money. Everything, you remember, costs money. Even Mum. Her nail varnish remover smells like pear drops and stings at where you've chewed at the skin around your thumbs. You sing 'My Camera Never Lies' with the wooden end of the skipping rope in front of the full-length mirror in your mum's bedroom until your mum flicks the trip and plunges the house into quiet. Your tea is on the table. You never do as you're told and you're the oldest, Dee. Set an example because I've got to go to work. And as she puts on her lipstick like she's chewing a wasp she tells you again: You're too clever for your own good and you're wasting it already because Cheryl Baker isn't even Cheryl Baker. Her real name's Rita Crudgington and don't ever forget who you are.

You are nine years old. You have a birthday party and invite all the girls from your class. Pass the parcel. Pin the tail on the donkey. Musical bumps, because the house is too small for musical chairs. And you don't have enough chairs anyway. Oonagh Macnamara gives you a birthday card and no present. Inside the card it says *I do not like you and I do not like your house, it smells. Love Oonagh.* She watches your cheeks burn as you read it. The picture on the front is of Victoria Plum. She tells you it's a card for babies and you think she's so cool and wish you could be best friends. She sits on the edge of your settee with her arms folded. Pass the parcel is for babies.

Musical bumps is for babies, and why haven't you invited any boys? Then she flounces towards the stereo and demands: *What's this crap?* You tell her it's Bucks Fizz and sing: *If you can't stand the heat, keep out of the kitchen. If you can't stand the cold, don't sleep on the floor.* She wants to see your bedroom so you show her.

You share a bedroom with your two sisters Sasha, who's five, and Colette, who's not yet four. You have three beds all in row with Care Bear duvet covers that you are too old for. It goes Funshine, Daydream and Love-a-lot bear. You sleep with your duvet cover inside out and tell your sisters stories about a bluebird called Bryony who's Welsh and slightly deaf. You can't remember if you told those stories with a Welsh accent, just that when it got to the parts when Bryony misheard something—'Trump, sir? Bluebirds don't trump! Oh dump! Yes, I agree. It's a right dump round here'—both your sisters would kill themselves laughing because according to them you are the funniest person in the world.

According to Oonagh you're the filthiest person in the world. 'And you've had the same trainers for ages,' she says, slamming the door on her way out.

Later, Mum asks why your trainers are in the bin. You blame Sasha and Sasha blames Colette. Sasha gets shouted at and bawls. So does Colette. You lock yourself in the bathroom and clean your teeth until your gums bleed and your toothbrush looks like you've been scrubbing drains.

Mrs Chew, your teacher, introduces you to the Reverend Chew, her husband, who gives you a copy of the Holy Bible. The cover is made of white satin wallpaper and the words 'Holy Bible' are stitched in silver. Inside, on the front page, someone has written 'I shall never question who I am'. It's only now that you realise what a grand percentage of your life you have wasted in doing exactly that, but turn that house upside down and you will never find that bible. That is gone too.

When you are ten you are still the eldest of three. It goes Mum, you, Sasha and Colette. You are doing your maths homework. Your mum says: if one man has two apples and another has three, and as your mum counts the apples you count the men. Then she tells you that you're getting a new baby for Christmas which will make you five. You yell, 'How? Why?' but that's another thing your mum says you're too young to understand.

So you tell her that you do understand because Oonagh Macnamara has drawn you a picture in your maths book: a stick-man with a line between his legs that pokes at a stick-lady's tuppence. You've told Oonagh that everyone knows that babies come out of your bellybutton which unravels and opens up like a flower, but Oonagh pointed to the stick and said, 'A million of them have poked your mum.' She also tells you that there's no Santa and no tooth fairy and that's why you've got such disgusting yellow teeth, 'Hooker spawn,' is what she said.

The new baby arrives on Christmas Eve so Christmas gets all forgotten. You only eat Quality Street because Santa got to your house last and had run out of wrapping paper and new tellies. You get Bucks Fizz Greatest Hits which you play on repeat. Side 1. Side 2. Side 1 again. Your mum calls the new baby Iona without asking any of you if that's OK. You never get told who her dad is, though Iona asks and asks and all through her life until she and Mum stop speaking completely and she doesn't even come to the funeral. But you know it's not your dad or Sasha's dad because you'll never meet them, and it can't be Colette's because he'll be in prison soon for robbing your old telly. So it goes Mum, you, Sasha, Colette and Iona, and you do not get that battery-operated toothbrush for Christmas even though it was the only thing on your list.

You're leaving school for the next one. You have to go and see the headmaster, Mr Aliss, and your mum is sat in his office wearing a man's overcoat and you hope that she's got more than underwear on underneath. You instantly think your nan's died. She's in a home called Cheddleton that you tell no one about because it's the funny farm. When you go she tells you that you should care for nothing but boys and petticoats and calls you our Ruthie which you're not. She squeezes your hand so tight all your knuckles go white and says, 'They're robbing me, Ruthie. They think I don't know. But I do. They're robbing me blind.' And even though you're not our Ruthie, because that's your mum, and your nan has nothing to rob because her room is bare and just white, you tell her that you'll take her home where she can squeeze in with you and one of the nurses has to come and prise your fingers from hers.

So you offer to leave school and look after her. Mum looks at Mr Aliss and goes, 'What! With your brains? Are you mad?' But you're not mad, not ever, and you're not a troublemaker either or ever going to turn out like Mum. You're not entirely sure what it is you do that the other girls don't like but you tell Mr Aliss, 'I'm trying really hard not to be clever.'

Mr Aliss says you've one hour to do the exam. He makes you do it in a classroom all on your own. The clock on the wall is MASSIVE and it ticks even LOUDER and you write in time to the tick and the tock, the tick and the tock, and when you've finished you realise that you've written most of your answers in rhyme. And they seem to be the right answers too.

The next headmaster you meet walks with a stick and says it's going to be super. You have to meet him on Tuesday for a look around the new school and as you wait for Tuesday to arrive, Sasha has to tell you a million times that it's not a hospital, you won't be getting a stick and you're not going mad, and don't you get it? Not only are you the funniest person in the world, but the brainiest too.

You start the Grammar School with a briefcase and Rick Astley on your walls. You've won a scholarship to be here and your uniform's second hand. You've been given a briefcase by your mum and your sisters because that's what they think girls in private schools on scholarships have. You sneak out of school one dinnertime and run into town to buy a pump-bag with a month's worth of pocket money you've been saving up. You keep this pump-bag in your briefcase and transfer all your books and pens into it when you get to school. Then you roll up your skirt and leave the briefcase in the senior cloakroom because you're sick of the girls calling you 'briefcase'.

'Oi, briefcase!' they go, and don't pick you for their netball team even though you've been given a county trial. So you make mistakes in your homework so you only get a C, and collect Grolsch bottle tops from pub bins so you can wear them on your Docs like Bros. 'But you don't even like Bros,' says Bryony Bluebird, and you're surprised to hear her voice because you'd thought you'd lost her for good. You still make Sasha buy the Bros album with her Christmas money and keep it in your pump-bag so that every now and then you can let it fall to the floor and everyone can see that you're just like them. You also keep hoping that the briefcase will get stolen, but it doesn't because your mum's a slag and shit breeds shit and scum like you from down the Abbey have no place being at a school like this. So you spend a lot of time hiding in that senior cloakroom with your briefcase because that way you won't speak with your fists.

You don't really fancy Rick Astley. You only put his poster up because you've got to fancy someone and, according to

Libby Lymer, use your tongue. So you stick Rick Astley over your Bucks Fizz posters but only with Blu Tack so you don't spoil them because everything costs money. Even Mum. Then you try and sit next to Libby Lymer because she has the most beautiful set of felt tips you have ever seen. 'Tits?' says Bryony Bluebird. 'I'm a bluebird not a tit!' and your sisters kill themselves laughing as you cuddle up as four, because your mum works at a gentleman's club now and has bought you two double beds with her tips.

You and Libby Lymer are best mates. She takes you up town and introduces you to Ant. He asks what you do and you say you go to school *durrr!* and he says, 'No. What will you *do*?' Because slags breed slags and 'If you won't do it with me, your mum will,' he says. So you punch him in the kidneys and then run for your life which was also the one Bucks Fizz song you never liked.

You do a silly thing to fit in. You let on to Libby Lymer that your mum works at the Velvet Rope. You're in Libby's bedroom listening to INXS at the time and she has a life-size poster of Michael Hutchence on her wall. Heart-throbs, your mum would say. Think of them as heart-throbs. Everyone has one of them on their walls.

Because that's what Mum had said after you'd met that man coming down the stairs. You'd got home in time to meet him coming down your stairs and you'd been struck by how ordinary he was. A man just in jeans and a shirt and shoes; he was wearing brown lace-up shoes. He didn't flinch when he saw you. Walked straight past you and out of the door as if you weren't there at all. Perhaps you weren't. It's possible that you've made that up too.

Libby Lymer chucks a camera at you, whips off her top and poses in front of Michael Hutchence's crotch. It's a Polaroid camera, and the Polaroid that comes out is blurred because your hands were shaking and you weren't really looking through the lens. So you're instructed to snap her again, and again, until there's no Polaroids left and Libby gives you the best one and tells you to give it to your mum to take to the Velvet Rope in case it's good enough for Page 3: because don't you know that Page 3 girls earn shitloads? And if you're too scared to say what you want, you won't ever get what you want. 'That's what Madonna says,' she says.

But you don't give the Polaroid to your mum and keep it in your briefcase instead so no one from the Velvet Rope ever calls Libby Lymer. And because you've let her down, she tells a teacher that you've a topless photograph of her and your briefcase is searched and the Polaroid found.

All the while you got asked all those questions you sung 'My Camera Never Lies' in your head and you tell them that *there's nothing worth lying for*. Except for Mum. Which you do: 'She's a hairdresser,' you say, 'who cuts men's hair.'

You become fascinated by Page 3 girls after that and start to collect them like stamps. You're fascinated by Linda, by Melinda, Samantha, Maria, their beauty, their guts, the size of their pearls, and you have three full scrapbooks by the time social services confiscate them, and you never see them again. All you ask is that they keep them protected like you have done, those girls. 'They need protecting,' is all you will say.

The social worker is called Mrs Incavich and when she talks her mouth barely moves. You lie down in the passenger seat of her car so no one sees you and she also drives a Skoda. You're not allowed to go to anyone's house after school and so Mrs Incavich drives you in and drives you home. And though you've said, and said again, that Libby Lymer made you do it because she wanted to be on Page 3, they're worried about your fascination with boobs. You try and explain that it's nothing to do with the boobs. You kind of get that bit.

Your new bedroom is so big you can cry yourself to sleep and not be heard. Sylvia and John—they're alright, you suppose—say you can stay as long as you like and your sisters come on Saturdays but go to their new homes on Sundays, and sometimes you all get to see Mum and go home. 'We'll get through this,' says Mum, when you have to say goodbye. 'And *you* will go to university, Dee.' Which you do.

Because Sylvia and John know someone who knows someone whose husband is a professor and you are sent to see him to see just how good you are, but the questions he asks you to answer are bizarre. They're not normal questions like 'Discuss the historical importance of the Bayeux Tapestry' and you ask if you have the right paper. The professor tells you it's a test of your thinking skills and that if we don't find new thinkers we'll never be able to think the world otherwise. So you go back to the paper and write about your own tapestry. You realise just how little of your life is actually yours and how so much of it doesn't belong to you. You share that part with Sasha and all of that with Colette and some of that with Iona and most of it with Mum, and though you remember the men that used to come and go and come and go, how your mum reassured you that they never used your bed, you cannot understand why a woman who's a mother—*your mum*—would ever want to go any further than Page 3.

You call your essay 'The Land of Make Believe' and you write it in pencil because pencil doesn't last. You don't ever get told if you've passed or if you'd made any spelling mistakes. Just that there was a place for you. Everything paid. And you go, just shy of your eighteenth birthday. Four A levels already in the bag.

~

You leave for Cambridge with a holdall, an attitude and acne so bad you're on medication that makes you weep. You use make-up from the Avon catalogue that your mum buys on tick and, though it tones down the embarrassment, it doesn't hide you away. Colette says you'll never get a boyfriend looking like you're part of a fry-up but Sasha tells you not to mind. 'She's just going to miss you,' she says. 'You're our big sister Dee.'

Sasha says she won't miss you. 'I'm too old for all that,' she says and won't even give you a hug. But when you get to Cambridge and open your holdall you find that she's put a £5 Woolworth's voucher in a good luck card for a 'trigonometry set or something' that you don't ever spend.

You last six months at Cambridge. You read Greer and Rich and De Beauvoir and Plath. You're appalled when Greer instructs you to taste your own blood; furious with Plath, for giving in, for giving up, for putting up with Ted, at their bleating, their squawking at the tyranny of the dick, and you stand up in a lecture and say, 'It's not being other to man that's the problem. It's other women and those who have no choice.'

The lecturer asks you to expand on that: she's particularly interested in your use of the word 'choice', which she warns you must not use flippantly. So you say, 'I can if I'm the daughter of a prostitute,' and, as everyone gapes, you push all those silly books to the floor and leave.

You hitch-hike to a service station and get talking to a woman who's going north. It's a three-hour drive and you talk all the way and say more than you've ever said in your life. You tell her that your mum's been a hooker for as long as you can remember but you don't ever talk about it, you're not a family of women programmed to talk about it, so you don't know why she does it or how she does it, just that you knew not to ask any questions and tell many lies. 'We're all just products of sex,' you tell the woman who's going north. 'And everyone knows that sex sells.'

After she's dropped you at the bus station, you find a café and order tea like a grown-up and think of your mum and your nan. You think of them as a mum and a daughter and then as two little girls playing mummies in the park. You have never asked your mum anything of her life. That all you have ever wanted to know is that she is mum to you, to Sasha, to Colette and Iona and that there's men, plenty of men, who come and go and come and go, and you've never had the bottle to ask her why: *Why, Mum? Why is sex your job?*

So you buy a bottle of Buck's Fizz as a joke and decide you will ask her today. She's surprised to see you but she opens the bottle anyway because she's an interview at four—'Nothing fancy, just answering the phones'—and as she chinks your glass and asks why you're here you realise that answering the phones is a demotion. That there are other girls now—younger, prettier, more in demand—and though she hasn't been entirely discarded, her body's become cheaper and old.

So you tell her you will apply for the jobs—secretarial, receptionist, checkout—and then give them to her. She slugs down her Buck's Fizz as if it were tea and says, 'I'm still a woman, Dee. I'm still working as a woman and I still want to be a woman and it is still happening.' And because she thinks you don't understand, she adds, 'Being a woman has been my job in this life and like anyone who's worked hard at their job, I, too, am good at it.' And when you open your mouth to protest that you *do* understand, that womanhood and motherhood are jobs in themselves, she shushes you with her fingers and beckons you to the stereo to press play. 'This is your chance to be somebody else, Dee,' she says. 'So don't go and spoil it by not being you.'

But you don't press play.

'I'm not a baby any more,' is what you said. 'You might see carnality as your job, but if you think objectifying yourself for men makes us equal then you live in a land of make believe.'

You'd pressed fast forward on that tape player and held it down until Bucks Fizz's Greatest Hits unspooled.

You go back to Cambridge and do all that you're told. You date no men—though there is one who keeps your lipstick-stained fag-butts in a tin—and you make few friends, none of whom you're ever straight with. You become outraged by the cavorting on the telly, by the skew-whiff feminism that has rag-clad pop stars talk of sexual choices and empowering their desires by skimping on their clothes. You're appalled by posters of padded-out Wonderbras, revolted by Madonna's *Sex*, and you write and write to Linda, to Melinda, to Samantha and Maria and urge them to put a stop to Page 3. We want role models not models, you write. And it's not ever about the boobs because you get that bit. Your dissertation opens with the 1981 Eurovision song contest and you ask who really won after Cheryl Baker's skirt got ripped off? And though you get a first and an MA scholarship which you take and then a PhD offer which you decline, because what you want to discuss has no theory, you tell your mum none of this because she can't be part of your world if you're ever going to make it as you.

She writes only once to tell you that you've broken her heart, and inside the card is the little gold locket that she's stopped wearing to give to you. You look at it and want your own locket. One that hasn't been around anyone's neck. You think of the amount of hands that have held it, the value it no longer has, and so you put it back into the envelope and reseal it, post it back with the words: 'Why couldn't you buy me a new one? Something that's for me and just from you.' But you never get a reply, just as you never would admit that what you hated most about university was that little room of your own and all that space to yourself.

Some time after Cambridge, you travel alone to New Zealand—it's as far away as you can possibly get—and you're over on the baggage by 16kg. You have your cards read by a woman called Maureen Fitzpatrick who does you a reading at her dining-room table as if it's the most normal thing to do in the world. She holds your hand and tells you that whatever's in your head does not rule your heart and that if you can't forgive then forget. She tells you to write it all down in a letter and burn it on a clean white saucer with a new white candle and that what you are doing here was not at all what you were after. Then she flips over a tarot card and says she can see you buying cushion covers with your mum. 'Homemaking,' she says. 'Settling down, putting down roots.' You call her a charlatan and leave.

The next day you join a coach tour of the North Island because you'd always wanted to walk on the Ninety Mile Beach. You do so with a girl called Jen who was born in Ripon but moved to Brazil when she was twenty-one because she used to lie awake at night thinking of all those parties going on in Copacabana without her. By the time you had to get back on the coach you still had eighty-nine miles to go with Jen still trying to convince you that you were more likely to lie on your deathbed wishing you'd had more sex than none at all.

You take a job in a shoe shop for a while. Women customers mainly, those who shopped for their better halves by saying, 'Oh I know his shoe size by wearing his slippers to the dustbin.' You catch the bus home to the wrong side of Auckland and only have to look at everyone's shoes in order to judge their lives feet up. Though you make a point of spitting on every brown lace-up you see.

You fly home shortly after and start to write your letters which you decide you should not burn. Instead, you send them to a publisher because if you can't beat 'em, join 'em and sex, after all, sells.

Later, much later, when Bryony Bluebird is a franchise about the rise and fall of a call girl who did it all for the girls in her life, you brush your teeth with a newfangled electronic toothbrush that's been designed by a Harley Street orthodontist especially for you. And though you and the orthodontist are dating and you're trying ever so hard to finally have sex, you neither make the date nor finish brushing your teeth because that's your sister on the phone with the news that you've been dreading.

Sasha wears black. Colette's in jeans and Iona doesn't turn up. In the front pew it goes writer, secretary, psychiatric nurse, and if Iona was here, nanny, because you're defined by each other and shaped by your past and you all do what women will do. You cry not for your mother or because she was just fifty-nine, but because not one of those men came to mourn her.

'Who was she?' you ask as the coffin disappears, and Sasha shrugs and says, 'Well who are you?' because she never knows what to put on your Christmas cards. 'Are you Bryony still Delilah or what?' And you tell her 'My other, like you're another,' and that she who is weakened by men becomes her own downfall. Sasha just laughs and reaches for your hand. 'Let her rest in peace, Dee,' she says. 'She was just a happy hooker, that's all.'

You pay for an extra week's rent because you can't bear clearing out your mother so quickly. But you don't need the extra week because your mother didn't have anything to leave. So you take the bus up to Cheddleton because you've got the job of telling your nan. She says, 'It's a mother's greatest fear, their child going before them,' and you watch her shrink into the armchair she never leaves and puzzle over her hands.

'Are these mine?' she asks. 'Because mine were ever so beautiful. First thing a man would say was what lovely hands I had. I'd say, "Well, there's the price list, duckie, so where can you afford these lovely hands to go?"' And you watch her hoot with laughter. 'You live off men whether you like it or not, Ruthie,' she carries on. 'So pity the mother not the whore.'

You take a taxi home and stand in front of the full-length mirror in your mum's bedroom, that little gold locket still fast about your neck. There's no skipping rope and no Bucks Fizz but you use your thumb and know all the words. You notice your thumb is bleeding from where you've chewed at the skin and as you look for cotton wool you realise there never was any scholarship. It was you who cost the money: Mum who betrayed you all for money, then had the nerve to call you Delilah. But then there is no 'I' in being women. Only *we*, and never *you*, and so you lie on your mum's bed and trace it all back: to £5 worth of Woolworth's vouchers you don't spend for a year.

Chuck and Di

DI IS IN HER KITCHEN PEELING POTATOES AT THE SINK. IN FRONT OF HER IS THE KITCHEN WINDOW WHICH LOOKS OUT ONTO A SMALL BACKYARD. THERE IS A SHED, TOO BIG FOR THE YARD, AND IT STOPS THE KITCHEN FROM GETTING ANY LIGHT. BEHIND HER IS A TABLE WITH TWO CHAIRS: THE TABLE SET FOR ONE.

I'd found it in his shed. Sat on his good toolbox it was with the price tag left on. Minton. Grasmere. Forty pieces. Five hundred quid all boxed up never used. Not ever going to be either.

Course, there was no way I could've said anything. I shouldn't have been in there in the first place. I could've said I was getting the emergency chairs out ready for Sunday, what with his sister and her brood coming for their dinners. And we all know what Chuck's sister's like when she's sat on my three-piece airing her views after a couple of her afternoon sherries, as we all know Chuck won't be able keep his trap shut when he's got a chance to play the martyr. But there was no point going down that road when I'd been promising Monica I'd turned a corner.

I still called Monica to tell her what I'd found. She told me to breathe—*breathe, Di, in, out, in, out*—then asked me where he was.

I said, 'You know where he is. I should kick the bloody door down.'

She said, 'Blind eye, Di, and keep your fists in the suds.'

I said, 'Monica, it's a spare room is that. Not a bloody museum. And that's another forty-piece dinner service he's just bought.'

She said, 'I'd be careful about who you're telling when you call it a spare room. If the council get wind you'll have to find yourself a lodger.'

I said, 'I'm already a housekeeper to a landlord.'

She said, 'Well just remember what happened last time. You meet him halfway.'

Because last time this happened there was no halfway. Wedgwood Florentine Blue it was. Beautiful to look at but it cleaned us out and broke my heart.

I said, 'What the hell were you ever thinking, Chuck, buying that lot?'

He said, 'Di, however hard you cherish them you've got to be prepared for discoloration in a dinner service. And trends. Grasmere. Persian Rose. Florentine Blue. They're in and out of fashion like a dipper's drawers. You need replacements just in case.'

I said, 'Doulton, Minton and Wedgwood, Chuck. No one gives a damn about men like you any more or for what you made. And while we're on the subject, cherish *me*.'

He went all doe-eyed on me then. His big left eye watering as he started wittering on about some article in *The Telegraph* he'd read about how a generation of collectors were dying off; everything royal losing its sparkle.

'No respect any more,' he said. 'Even Cameron was late seeing our Queen.'

And because I'd upset him, he went and spent the whole day with his collection, dabbing at their faces all tender with that rubbery chamois he'd paid the earth for, wrapping them up again, putting them away. Then he came out of his room, all sunshine and smiles with newspaper print and somebody else's stories all over his hands, except he was heading for my armchair.

I said, 'Whoa, Daddy, whoa! Not on my cream armchair you don't,' because his hands were as black as the night.

He sat down anyway, all defiant, strumming his fingers on my cushions. It was no wonder I saw red.

But he'd started it.

He always does.

DI PUTS THE POTATOES INTO A SAUCEPAN AND PLACES THEM ONTO THE STOVE. IT IS ONLY FOUR O'CLOCK BUT THE KITCHEN IS DARK. SHE WIPES HER HANDS ON A TEA TOWEL, FLICKS ON THE LIGHT AND GOES TO SIT DOWN AT THE KITCHEN TABLE.

The thing about my Chuck is that, once upon a time, he had a hand in making all those crocks. He used to bring them home—'porcelain babes' he'd call them—and they'd be as warm as rock cakes out the oven. He'd show our boys, tell them how it'd been made from clay to oven from dip to glost—I can see him now on his whirly stool with his magnifiers, that pencil-thin brush of his steady-as-she-goes as he enamelled around the rim. He was a fine looker back then, all dapper and natty, shirt, tie and waistcoat every day of his life—flashing me a wink with his big left eye as I went for my break with the girls.

'He's got his eye on you again, Di,' nudge, nudge, wink, wink. 'Never lets you out of his sight.'

Should've known then. Shouldn't I?

Course, he'd only have to pass me on the stairs and I was pregnant. And in them days being a mother was your job so I never went back the factory after we were wed.

Anyway, we ticked along until Charles and Di went and tied the knot. And believe me when I say it, it was a true fairy tale for the likes of us. That much work on we nearly went Tenerife for us holidays. Except Chuck went and fell. Patch of black ice down the Dividy Road. Broke his right wrist and snapped the bone that bad it mended with a kink that used to shiver when he held a brush. Shop steward offered him no end of jobs. You could do this, Chuck. You'd be blinding at that. He said, 'I were blinding at bloody gilding,' and he were on the sick for the best part of a year. Couldn't get out of bed. Wouldn't see a soul. Then they stopped his money. I started losing my temper because folk were talking.

'You can fix a broken wrist, Di,' he'd say. 'But not a broken mind.'

And I'd look at Lady Di's face on his mug of tea and think —I hadn't a clue for what I was getting myself into either, duck, though it's written all over my face in the wedding photographs; Chuck's sister stood aside of him wearing her bloody claret and all mouth. It was a bit too crowded even then. My mother said, 'I don't like the look of her, Di. Face like a bag of spanners with one eye on her brother all the bloody while. They're watchers that family. On the lookout for themselves.'

But that was my mother for you. Never saw the good in no one. Like I said to her as me and her watched Chuck overanalysing the gilding on our wedding crockery, 'A true potter flips over a plate and checks where it's been born. Rare breed my Chuck. One in a bloody million.'

'Then keep your fists in your pockets and your kicks in your head if you want him kept,' my mother said, tapping her nose like she did. 'And don't give up work either. Because men like that won't keep a woman like you for all the crocks in bloody China.'

Pause.

Chuck was just shy of his sixty-fifth when his brother-in-law went and died out of the blue. Carked it on the bathroom floor from a fatty liver. Course, Chuck's sister was over the moon because he was that much in debt she was having to take blood pressure tablets. Liked a flutter, you see. He had a tab that big down the bookies it took all his insurances clean his slate. He'd have been buried in cardboard if it wasn't for us. Not a single hymn, of course. One of them humanist affairs. Robbie Williams on cassette. 'Angels'. Volume turned up like it was a disco.

I said, 'I'm sorry, Nora. I know you didn't love him but he was your husband.'

She said, 'Husband? We've lived separate lives for over thirty years. Not all of us got as lucky as you.'

Except Chuck took it real hard. Disappeared from the funeral and didn't come home till the Saturday. Three days he was gone. I'd almost got the police dredging the canal.

I said, 'If I wanted to live with a lodger I would've advertised for one. Where the bloody hell have you been?'

He said, 'I've been ruled by us past for far too long now, Di, and let you get away with blue bloody murder.'

And straight off he took charge like I'd never seen. Told me he'd retired early, walked away with what pension was in the pot and spent a bit of it already.

I said, 'You've done what?'

'Computer,' he said. 'I've retired and bought a computer.'

He took over the spare room. Wires going all up my walls, Argos lorry outside the house ferrying in cabinets. That's without mentioning the credit cards.

I said, 'What fool has given you those?'

He said, 'Banks like you spending, Di. It's how they make their money.'

But when I went down the bank to have a word I got told that the cards weren't anything do with me. No payments coming from our account—I'm sorry, Mrs Windsor. But your husband must've opened a separate account.

So I tackled him that night. Said, 'What are you doing having your own bank account? I thought me and you shared everything?'

He said, 'My pension, Di. I'll spend it how I want.' Then says I've done nowt more with my life than live off him. Said I'd have his wages spent before he even got them home. Cleaned him out with my fancies and whatnot.

I said, 'If it were left up to you, Chuck, I'd have lived a sparse little life with not so much as a dolly peg to call my own.'

But that's the thing about peacocks. They don't flash their feathers to mate. They're just reminding you who rules the roost.

DI TAKES OUT A BAG OF FROZEN PEAS FROM THE FREEZER AND REMOVES A MEAT AND POTATO PIE (HOMEMADE) FROM THE FRIDGE. SHE SETS ABOUT PUTTING THE PEAS INTO A PAN, THE PIE IN THE OVEN. SHE THINKS ABOUT HALVING THE PIE, HOVERS OVER THE CRUST WITH A KNIFE. BUT THINKS BETTER OF IT, PUTS THE WHOLE PIE IN THE OVEN AND SITS BACK DOWN.

He put locks on the door of the spare room. Bolt on the inside. Yale lock on the outside. I hardly ever saw him. Months went by. I packed a bag in the end. Told him a fib. Said I was going in the City General for some tests.

I said, 'This secret life of yours, Chuck. It's making me ill.'

He said, 'It was meant to be a surprise.'

I said, 'Only surprise I want is to know I'm not dying and you've not lost your marbles.'

He opened the door then. 'Nest egg,' he said. 'What do you think?'

It took me quite a while to tell him that I couldn't believe my bloody eyes.

Most of it was Charles and Di memorabilia—ashtrays, thimbles, commemorative plates and mugs, but there were other pieces, prize pieces, that he'd bidded for on the computer. And then there was the rest of it: anything that'd been fired in Stoke. It were like a car bloody boot sale in there all laid out. I thought—I've given this man forty-one years of my life and three sons, hot dinner every night, kept the house nice, never once thought about leaving, and he wants me to appreciate this?

'This is our destiny,' he said.

I said, 'I'll give you bloody destiny and ram it where the sun doesn't shine.'

And that's when it went and happened.

The bit when I didn't feel very lucky at all.

Pause.

Afterwards, he sat me down and told me that it was the last time.

I said, 'I know.'

He said, 'I mean it, Di.'

I said, 'I know. I heard you the first time.'

'Because next time I don't want to do something I shouldn't.'

I said, 'Alright, Chuck. You've made your point.'

He said, 'Have I, Di? Because I don't want it to happen again.'

I said, 'Alright, don't keep on.'

He said, 'I'm not on about you. I'm on about me. What I did.'

I said, 'I know. Do you want a cup of tea?'

He said, 'Because I can't live with myself, Di, if it happens again. Do you understand?'

I said, 'Yes. Now go and wash your face. There's some plasters in the cupboard.'

He said, 'I don't know what you want, Di, but I can't keep on like this.'

I said, 'A holiday would be nice. Somewhere abroad. So I can send postcards.'

He said his sister knew someone—Monica he thought her name was—friend of the family. 'You should go see her,' he said. 'Have a word.'

Except he'd already made me an appointment. Anger management. Every Tuesday, ten o'clock, for ten weeks.

I said, 'What's that costing us?'

And he said, 'Exactly, Di. You're costing *us*.'

DI IS WEARING RED OVEN GLOVES. SHE CHECKS THE PIE, TURNS DOWN THE HEAT. THE PEAS ARE STILL SIMMERING, THE POTATOES ARE DONE. SHE DRAINS THEM, FETCHES MILK AND BUTTER OUT OF THE FRIDGE, CHECKS THEIR LABELS FIRST TO CHECK THEY'RE HERS, THEN BEGINS TO MASH.

She was American, the woman who bought it. I got her number from one of Chuck's collecting magazines. *Randy*, her name was. Sounded like she kept cats. Said she couldn't offer me what she'd offered a few months back because these type of collections were starting to lose their value and she could get it much cheaper if she bought from Canada.

I said, 'What do you mean, a few months?'

She said her and Charles had been trading crockery collectables now for the best part of a year and she was sure that, genealogically speaking, we were all related to the royals one way or the other. I thought, that'd be right, duck. Remind me of the life I didn't get because I wanted a man so tight he creaked. So I told her that some of the stuff was signed by the gilder himself, put the price up and wouldn't budge. She had the lot.

Charles. Only time my Chuck answered to Charles was when that young parson came to see him on the ward after he'd had his stomach pumped. *Charles.* Like I told him, 'You need to pull your bloody socks up, Chuck, and remember you're a dad.'

Pause.

A week on the *QE2* is what Chuck's crock collection bought me. Royal as you'll ever be made to feel and the bed linen is beautiful. Though I did think it was a bit much changing your towels every day. Not that I ever saw them peg out, even with all that sunshine, and we docked these couple of times, Valencia someone said, then somewhere opposite the Canaries, but I never got off. I'd paid to be on that boat all week and there was enough sights keep me busy on board. All I'll say is no quality control. Riff-raff isn't the word. Like I said to the bloke in the next-door cabin, flicking his fag-butts into the sea, 'There's fish in there, sunshine. Endangered species. Lifetime conscription's what you lot need, because a class like you doesn't know the meaning of bloody work.'

And he started goading me—people like you? What about people *like you*?—so I chinned him up the chops shut him up. Told him to have some bloody respect: I'm a pensioner still paying her way and my Chuck was a gilder to royal crocks. Except his wife came out of nowhere and knocked me flying. I went down like a stack of plates.

I don't think I've ever felt as lonely as I did when floored on that deck with everyone looking down on me. I cried my heart out actually.

DI IS SITTING DOWN AT THE KITCHEN TABLE WITH HER TEA IN FRONT OF HER: MEAT AND POTATO PIE WITH MASH AND PEAS. SHE HAS FORGOTTEN TO MAKE GRAVY. SHE CURSES AND MAKES A FIST WHICH SHE THUMPS DOWN ON THE TABLE. SHE DABS AT HER EYES WITH HER APRON. PICKS UP HER KNIFE AND FORK. PUTS THEM DOWN AGAIN.

Monica says that you might pop a pill and hope the headache will drift but you can't sedate a past and hope it won't remember you. I said, 'I'm a lot of things, Monica. My hands have done a lot of things, but I'm not a bad wife.'

She said, 'Did you send any postcards?'

I said, 'No. Not a one.'

She said, 'Why?'

I said, 'Forty-one years of marriage, three sons, hot dinner every night, I've kept the house nice, and never once thought about leaving.'

Pause.

'You've got a bit of colour in your cheeks,' Chuck said, and I clocked the white tape straight away. On the carpet it was, stretching between the rooms.

I said, 'What's all this, Chuck? It'll pull the pile.'

He said he'd been doing some careful thinking, what with me being away, and he'd had to make a decision.

I said, 'Is that us now, Chuck? Split in two?'

He said no. The council had been round. Heard a rumour that we'd got a spare room.

I said, 'What spare room?'

He said, 'That's what I said. But I put down the tape all the same,' and he went and shut himself in his room.

DI BEGINS TO EAT HER MEAL. SHE HAS HER MOUTH FULL. SHE TALKS TO THE PIE IN FRONT OF HER.

Course, we're as right as rain now. All forgotten.

'Still here, then?' I say when he comes out of his room of a morning looking old.

'I am,' he says. 'And so are you.'

And we meet halfway between the tape before going our separate ways.

DI CONTINUES TO EAT HER EVENING MEAL FADES OUT.

Hoops

Tuesday

Rae's in Bed 32 and we're the only people here. Mam's a fussing goose and still got her slippers on. 'Little duck,' she coos, and that's definitely a Colclough's chin. It's gone 2 a.m.

Rae's boyfriend Mo feels his chin. It's smothered in black whiskers except for a patch where his lips join on the left. There his skin's caramel smooth. Sometimes I can't keep my eyes off it. Mo's wearing his Stoke City shirt and he's showing Uncle Chalky the Stoke City babygro he's bought online. Uncle Chalky points to my new niece and goes, 'Babbie's a girl, Cleo,' and Mo looks hurt. Not because Uncle Chalky always calls him Cleopatra, but because football's for everyone. Boys and girls. Englands and Germans.

'You not like the football?' Mo says. He pretends to score a goal and punches the air.

Uncle Chalky drops his eyebrows and says to Mam, 'You sure he's got papers?'

Mam says, 'You want to be careful you don't *get in* the papers. If anyone sees you here.'

My sister butts in. 'You haven't said what you think of her?' and she gives me the baby.

I hold her like melting ice cream. 'Bit scrawny,' I say. 'Why are her nails black?'

Mo goes, 'Clawing.' He burrows with his hands into the bed sheets. 'Like her Dada had to do when he ran for his life.'

Uncle Chalky rolls his eyes. 'Ran into the right bloody life, didn't yer, mate?' he says. Mam gives him the look.

'Chalky,' she says. 'Don't start.'

And he goes, 'What have I said now? Free bloody country. He knows that.' He points at Mo.

Rae holds out her arms and I see she's only room for Mo and her baby now. There's not any room for me any more. 'She's hungry,' she says. 'You can give her back now.'

I watch Mo give Mam a kiss. 'Grandma,' he says, and Mam says no. 'Sitto,' she says. 'I'd like her to call me Sitto.'

As Mo bursts into tears, Uncle Chalky spits on his shoes and walks out.

Wednesday

Mam asks Mo if his family have been caught up in the latest fighting. Mo says he doesn't know. He's not spoken to his family in a long time and can't afford the phone calls because the lines have been diverted to government taps they must bribe for personal calls.

'I am scared for them,' he says. 'They're brotherhood people.'

Mam says the only brotherhood she's ever known is the Brotherhood of Man. *Save all your kisses for me,* she sings. Mo goes, 'We're not men like *that*, Sitto,' and walks out the room.

Rae's key-worker Lizzie says she should be off the list in six weeks' time if she can tick all the boxes. Rae said, 'Fucking boxes. Fucking hoops. It's no wonder I need a drink.'

The baby's eyes are wide open today. I wonder what she thinks of us all.

Saturday

Rae's had to move to a house for single new mams that's just around the corner. Rae's not agreed to live there but Mam says she has to because it's got round-the-clock staff and Lizzie will sweep her room three times a day: if there's drink, it'll be found and poured down the loo. Rae calls it prison and wants to come home. Mam said, 'Grow up, Rae.'

Mo was at the door of Rae's new place struggling with the new pram. It was a present from Social Services. Uncle Chalky went, 'Present from us soft-headed taxpayers more like'—and that's why he won't buy them a gift.

Uncle Chalky was a soldier but won't do it any more because of what's he seen, so now he's got all these things wrong with him. He shows me the pains but I can't see them because they're all in his mind and under his skin. I said, 'Tell me about the Gulf.' He said there's a gulf so wide between rich and poor, north and south that he's feels revolting even if he isn't. Mam said, 'You're too bloody idle to fill the kettle. I fought harder for a fag on the school field.'

I see that Mo's crying. 'They're tears of rage,' he says. 'My brotherhood die every day.' And he pats his cheeks with a baby wipe. 'I should be there, fighting. But I am here, living.'

I said, 'How many brothers do you have?'

He said, 'We're all brothers in terrorism. We all bleed red'—and he shows me his scars again. Those that were made with a knife before he left Egypt without asking. They don't look as cool as he thinks so I said, 'I'm going up to see Rae.' But as I get to the door I hear Lizzie telling Rae that if she finds vodka again she'll have that baby off her like a shot.

Monday

Uncle Chalky and Mo have been wetting the baby's head and celebrating Mo's birthday. He is twenty-seven. Mo was so drunk Mam let him sleep in the bath. Uncle Chalky said he was telling Mo not to go home to fight. 'I don't trust him, Jean,' he said. 'He's one of them. I know it.'

Mam dropped tears into the cups of coffee she kept making. 'You just don't like being a grown up,' she said. 'Did anyone see you together?'

Mam's had another letter from Housing telling her that the bungalow we were getting got given to someone who didn't need three bedrooms and that maybe she should think about finding somewhere just for herself.

Wednesday

Rae and Mo have named the baby Isis Jean which means Queen Jean if you're Egyptian. Mam cried when they told her. Jean's been in the family donkeys. Uncle Chalky called it slap-in-the face defiance.

'We're no longer a single currency, Jean,' he shouted at Mam. 'You've let us be spiked.'

Mam said, 'Don't think I won't make a phone call, Chalky. You might be my brother but I'm not afraid of doing what's right,' then ordered him out of her sight.

Isis weighs 9lb 1oz and is on the 50th centile which means things are very normal but it doesn't feel that way at all.

Thursday

Uncle Chalky's in his room 'occupying'. If I ask him what else he's doing, he goes, 'Wiring.' But he might be saying, 'Worrying.' I'm not sure.

I helped bath Isis today. Rae says that if they lived in Egypt Isis would be bathed in the Dead Sea.

I said, 'No she wouldn't. Egypt has taps.'

That made Mo laugh so much he cried.

Friday

Josie from Housing came over to show Mam some photographs of bungalows on her computer that she has to bid for. Apparently we have to plead our case and make it sound good. Mam put her head in her hands and asked Josie how she slept at night.

'A stiff drink or two,' she said and then apologised. 'Sorry, Jean, I didn't think.'

Then she asked me why I wasn't in college again. 'Baby-sitting,' I said.

Josie said that Mam would have more luck with one-bedroom places and to remember that I was nineteen.

Mam said, 'I've already lost one daughter to another world I don't understand so whether she's nineteen or ninety-three, she stays with me.'

Josie put away her computer and said she'd do her best.

Monday

Uncle Chalky hasn't been out of his room since Thursday. Mam hammered on the door and said, 'I hope you're not pissing on my carpets.' But Uncle Chalky never replied.

I knocked on the door and said, 'Uncle Chalky, talk to me.'

He said, 'I'm wiring/worrying'—and something about soldiering.

'He wants back in the army,' I told Mam.

She rolled her eyes and said, 'You've got to leave to want back in.'

Josie phoned Mam to tell her that another bungalow had come up. It's ten miles from where we live but has a bit of garden.

Josie said, 'This is a one-chance saloon, Jean. Think of how you're deteriorating.'

Mam said she'd discuss it with the family but she hasn't mentioned it to any of us yet.

Wednesday

Rae asked Mam to babysit so she and Mo could have a date. Mam said, 'Already? You're breastfeeding,' and Rae went, 'Give us a break, Mam. I'm knackered.' And so Mam relented as long as Rae promised all-night lemonades and then asked me to go get Isis's things.

When I got there, Mo was in Rae's room talking Urdu on his mobile. I don't understand Urdu. I still don't understand what he was doing in Rae's room without Rae and how he got in there. He cupped the phone against his ear and said, 'Rae in bath.'

I said, 'No she's not. She's round at Mam's. What you doing here?'

He put the phone away and said it was rude to eavesdrop on other people's lives, especially when you don't understand why they have to live like they do. If I ever ask Mo about his Egyptian life he says it's an obligation he's turned his back on. 'I am guilty,' he says, and turns off the telly in case he sees someone he knows being shot. If I ever ask Mam about what she knows about Mo's Egyptian life she just says, 'They don't want to be ruled by our God,' but she doesn't really know about foreign governments. She just listens to Jeremy Vine.

Mo was still cupping his phone. I said, 'Aren't you and Rae going out tonight?'

He looked confused and said, 'Yes.'

I have given him the benefit of doubt because new parents can't even remember putting the kettle on they're that tired.

Thursday

Isis cried all night for Rae. Mam rang her mobile fifty-three times until Isis fell asleep then Uncle Chalky crept out of his room and stared at the baby for a very long time. Then he woke up Mam.

'I said you'd end up her mother if she had her,' he seethed, and he was poking a long stretch of smouldering wire near her eyes. 'There'll be other daughters, Jean. Egyptian mummies in every room. Do you really want to see all that?'

Mam called him a racialist and to remember Iraq.

Uncle Chalky said he didn't want to remember Iraq and that's why he was going to stick the soldering wire in his eyes. 'Won't want me back if I can't see shit,' and then he screamed so loud I thought my ears would burst.

It's funny because Isis has blue eyes and both Rae and Mo have brown.

Friday

Mam and Rae had an almighty bust-up about Rae and Mo stopping out all night. 'That was a heartbroken baby thinking it'd been abandoned,' Mam yelled. 'She's three weeks old, Rae, and this is motherhood.'

Later, I asked Mam if motherhood and Mo's brotherhood were fighting for the same sort of thing—'You know, like how to bring up babies properly'—but she just asked the Lord to give her some strength and a nice new kidney.

Mo turned up later with a bunch of chrysanthemums from the Costcutter. Mam made him a coffee and said she'd seen a couple of jobs in the paper. They're looking for trainee bus drivers, the route is their estate.

'You need to look on the website.' She points to the computer.

'I will look another day,' he says.

Mam held onto his arm. 'You're a father now,' she said. 'That's your obligation. Rae and the baby, that's your responsibility. Your life is here now, and I need to live somewhere without stairs. My kidneys are packing in.'

Mo told Mam that the important things in his life are being taken care of very well.

'I'd murder for my family, Sitto,' he says.

Uncle Chalky is still in his room wiring/worrying/soldering/soldiering. I change his eye bandage three times a day and give him a pill for the pain.

Saturday

Rae came over this morning in a flap. Isis had a rash, was really hot, and we could smell the drink on Rae's breath. Mam laid her fingers across Isis's forehead.

'She isn't hot,' she said. 'She's wearing too many clothes.'

As Mam undressed Isis, Isis kicked Mam in her Colclough's chin. 'I know,' Mam told Isis. 'This is a horrible world for you.' Then she shouted at Rae, 'Why did you put her in so many clothes?'

Rae says she didn't. Then she slurred, 'I dressed her, I asked Mo to dress her, maybe I dressed her again'—but Isis was wriggling about in her nappy, happy as Larry. Rae says, 'Would you mind her while I'll go tell Mo she's fine?'

Mam says, 'No, Rae'—because we both knew where Rae really wanted to go and the taxi was here for Mam's dialysis.

Egypt is a war zone now. People are being killed left right and centre and yet people are still going there on holiday. Apparently, the diving is brilliant.

Wednesday

Lizzie told Rae that her and Mo can't go on the real housing list until she turns eighteen. Until then she must prove she can stay off the booze and do all the things the social workers want her to do for Isis. She's also got to retake her GCSEs and that means two days in college. Mam said, 'More hoops,' and called up Josie to say that she'd go and look at the bungalow with that nice bit of garden. Josie said it'd gone last week.

'I've been bidding all this time for no reason?' and Mam was so mad she put on her coat and told us all to get down the Town Hall and rally like they were doing in Egypt, fighting for work, for freer places to live, to not be ruled by the rich and corrupt and have their kids grow up as snipers or living off bins in the street. 'My kidneys are giving up but I'm not,' she shouted, and she kicked Uncle Chalky's leg because he's got an eye-patch now and doesn't know what's going on to his left. 'Come with me, Chalky. Help.' And she even used the word 'brotherhood'. But none of us could be arsed to get the bus down there, and anyway, it'd started to rain.

Monday

Mo's been working in London since Friday. Rae told us a friend of his has found him work and if he stays until next Friday he might get a permanent contract and come home at weekends.

'He's got to prove himself,' Rae said, but she was very vague about proving himself in what.

Wednesday

Rae asked me if I was still keeping my diary. 'Sometimes,' I said.

'Do you talk about me in it?' she asked.

I told her, 'Not really.'

'Then what's it about? Because you don't do anything. You never leave the house.'

I reminded her that I went to the shop on Monday.

She said, 'Come on, Lo. Let's go out properly. Me and you. We could go into town. Go to a club. I'll ask Mam to babysit.'

I glared at her. 'No,' I said.

'It's not going to happen again,' she said. 'I've hardly had a drink since Isis.' She stared down at the baby who was asleep on the rug by the telly. I don't tell Rae that I like to put that rug on my bed at night because it helps me to sleep. I like the smell Isis leaves on it. I sleep with it under my nose.

'Maybe,' I said.

Rae looked really happy about that because she said, 'Right. I'll ask Mam. Me and you will have a last blowout tonight.' Then she asked me if I had any money. I nodded. 'Of course you have,' she said. 'How much have you saved now?'

'£638,' I told her proudly.

'Wow,' she said. 'That's more than before.'

'I know,' I said. 'I want a new computer.'

She scooped up Isis. 'Hold her while I nip to the loo?'

I like holding Isis. When I do I don't feel a single thing. I'd hold her all day if I could. But then Rae was back and said she was going home to get some clothes.

'My glad rags,' she said, and then she kissed me on the cheek. She's never done that before. 'I'll see you in a bit,' she said. She held Isis in her arms and got me to cover her with a blanket to keep her warm. But Rae never came back and nor did Isis, so we never went out.

Friday

It's been two days since we last saw Rae. Lizzie came round to ask if we knew where she was. 'She's not at home,' she told Mam. 'And her mobile's dead.' She asks Mam if Rae has a passport.

Mam shook her head and said, 'But I spoke to her last night,' and she looked panicked.

Lizzie asked her to tell her about their conversation. 'How did she sound?'

'Fine,' Mam said. 'She was fine.'

'You know I'll have to call the police, Jean,' Lizzie said. She cocked her head towards Uncle Chalky's room. 'You might want to tell him before I do.'

Mam said we couldn't call the police because they'll come round the house and see Uncle Chalky even if he can't see them.

I said, 'No they won't. He locks his door.'

'They'll have a warrant,' she said. 'And they'll take your computer.'

I gripped onto it. 'Why would they want my computer?' I said. 'It's mine.'

'Nothing belongs to you any more,' she said. 'Not even this country.'

I'm sure Uncle Chalky shouted 'Hallelujah' from his room.

'They're not having my computer,' I said again, and I unplugged it from the wall and stuffed it in a pillowcase under my bed.

Before Lizzie went, Mam gripped onto her hand dead tight. 'Find her before she gets there,' she said. 'Because you're all to fucking blame.'

I've never heard Mam swear like that before. She's normally so ladylike.

Later, Mam told me that they'll take my computer because of the Internet. She said, 'That's the real terrorist,' and looked really pleased with herself as she said it.

Saturday

The police ransacked the house. They even found my computer under the floorboards. Mam was proper cross about that. 'What the hell are you doing putting it under there?' she yelled at me.

'Because you said they'd take it!' I shouted back.

'Well of course they'll bloody take it if you hide it under the floorboards!' and she looked like she really hated me. Then she hugged me. Really, really tight.

'Where is she, Lo?' she said. 'Where the hell has he taken her?'

I pulled away from her. 'Probably to the pub,' I said.

She slapped my face.

I have still not told her that Rae has taken my £638 that was under my bed.

Monday

Mo, Rae and Isis have now been missing for over a fortnight. The days feel longer than they should though the batteries in the kitchen clock have stopped. Mam has also stopped eating and drinking which is doing her kidneys no good. She says she doesn't care. Until Rae gets home she's on a hunger strike. That way Mo will know how serious she is.

Lizzie came round to ask if there'd been any news. Mam refused to get out of bed. So Lizzie called Josie. She knows Mam and Josie get on. Josie was on annual leave so Lizzie put her mobile on speakerphone. 'I'll come and see you, Jean, when I get back,' Josie said. 'I'm up in Liverpool at the minute shopping with my daughter for her university digs.'

Mam told her to fuck off. I've never heard her swear so much in my life. I sent Rae a text to tell her. And not to spend all my money on booze. But she didn't reply.

Friday

The policeman who came to tell us was with someone from the Armed Forces and someone from the government who looked really tired. There was also someone from Citizen's Advice and Lizzie came too because she said she had to be here because Rae was her client and she probably knew more about her and her needs than anyone else. Mam looked like she was going to sock her one for that, but I shouted, 'Don't put us in jail!' so she didn't.

'She's in Turkey,' was what they all came to tell us.

'And my granddaughter?'

The man from the government told us this bit. He didn't even flinch when Mam punched him in the kidneys and screamed.

Monday

Rae's in Bed 16 in a special hospital we can all live at for a bit until it's time to go home. There's a policeman outside the door and another one back at our house and because the hospital is on an army base you get to hear a lot of gunshot which makes it sound like we're at war. Mam holds Rae's hand and refuses to let go even though Rae won't speak to her. Rae has also refused to take off her clothes and headscarf which actually really suit her. Her face is all tanned and freckly. She looks just like she's been on holiday. Fallen in love. Gone diving. Had a good time.

Mam had to go for her dialysis so I stayed put with Rae. I was looking at how dirty her feet were when she suddenly spoke. But it was nothing major. Just that his other wives were really beautiful and she couldn't understand a word they said.

There was lots I could've asked her but I didn't. It's nice to have her back, even if she did spend all my money, but now Uncle Chalky's gone missing. If it's not one, it's the other, and we just keep going round in circles. I don't know how other families do it.

Prawn Cocktail

As a writer, I am expected to tell stories and make things up. Tonight was no exception when, halfway through a date, while sat at a table with a basket of sauce sachets and sticky with spilt drinks, I was asked if I could indeed make up a story on the spot from beginning to end.

Despite my protests, and that I didn't think stories really had ends, I said that the mainstay of this story is of a man and a girl who are having an affair in a town where there are no secrets. Though I would, if I had more time to think this through, set this against the backdrop of war like Kosovo, or even Iraq, because that might give these unlikely lovers context and I might even win a prize. But anyway. This man and this girl have had an affair that has gone on longer than it should because we meet this man and this girl not long after they have had a conversation about what happens next. The girl—and we will call her Janet, Janet Bone—says 'Isaac'—because that is to be the man's name in all of this, Professor Isaac Drinkwater—'Isaac. We need to talk about what happens next.'

Now I have Janet Bone wearing a white dress that is made of that jersey material that clings to your skin and makes you itch and it is as cheap and small as a paper napkin and looks it. Janet is also a student on a scholarship reading English. 'And scholarships are someone's investment.' Because now this a story about class, do you see how that has evolved? And sex. Education.

So Janet is telling Isaac yet again that she loves him: 'You know I love you, Isaac,' which she says at least ten times a day (this sort of reassurance stems from a doting mother who might indeed dote but has never had the guts to articulate it, though that's another story altogether). Isaac, on hearing that she loves him, looks up from the menu he has been studying—because it's time this story had a sense of place and they are in what one might call a bistro, and you are already imaging red and white gingham tablecloths with couples eating spaghetti by tea lights I'm sure—and he says, 'Do you think they'll do me a prawn cocktail? I could murder a prawn cocktail.'

'What about the whitebait?' Janet asks. 'You like whitebait.' She pauses. 'You used to like whitebait anyway.'

'I like prawn cocktail,' he replies and Janet sees that he's not joking. He is deadly serious that this is what he wants.

'Why can't you just order what's on the menu? There's plenty of fish to choose from.' Because Professor Isaac Drinkwater has a reputation, a wife and a wandering eye and Janet has often encountered old lovers, even dined with ex-bits on the side.

Isaac slaps the menu shut and beckons over the waitress he likes with the sweet potato hair. 'A prawn cocktail,' he declares as she arrives with her pad and Janet is amazed when she says, 'Of course.'

'You've had it here before?' Janet enquires, as Isaac reaches into his top pocket for his cigarettes. 'And must you smoke already?' Janet's tone is so cold it could sharpen the knives that lie blunt and under-washed on the table. 'We've only just sat down.' And she notices that there's a button missing on his shirt, that there's blood on his collar from a shaving nick, that he's chosen to not wear a tie. 'You never used to be this slovenly,' Janet says, and she holds up a napkin and gestures for him to blot his neck. But he doesn't take the napkin. Simply waves his mobile phone at her and mutters something about checking in with the death squad which Janet has never found funny. Then he turns and says, 'I'm with you, aren't I?' and Janet is forced to agree because he is.

Left with the waitress poised with her pad, Janet asks her, 'Do you know the professor well?'

Except the waitress mishears and asks, 'The professor isn't well?' and she asks Janet if she has made up her mind.

'No,' says Janet. 'I haven't.' And she asks the waitress for five minutes.

In that five minutes she takes out a pen and makes a list on the napkin that Isaac has refused. She writes with a fine black nib and though the ink bleeds quickly she sits back and reads:

1. *The years between / the years passed*
2. *He will never leave her*
3. *Nil by mouth from tomorrow*
4. *It's my body not his*

And whether it is because she has written them by candlelight or because she knows, deep in her pregnant gut, that those bleeding words are all true, it's right then that Janet Bone makes her decision. Which is why I thanked my date for a lovely evening, gave him my napkin and left.

In 2010, I was approached by the music journalist and photographer Kevin Cummins to contribute to an anthology by northern writers he admired. The brief was to respond to one of Kevin's photographs however we wished. I was sent this photograph — 'Bar Man'.

© Kevin Cummins

My response was to write a story about the smoking ban and its effects upon those who had worked in places synonymous with smoking. So I had my 'Bar Man' writing to the then sixteen-year-old Euan Blair, Tony Blair's son, who had been arrested for drunkenness in London after his GCSE exam results.

Love, Alvin and Ramona

DEAR EUAN, I wrote. Have a word with your dad, son. It's not the fags. It's the lack of future in general.

Love, Alvin and Ramona.

He never replied. He never has. But they came for me anyway. I said to them, 'Do you know who I am?' And I gave them me business card—Alvin Starr, Human Jukebox. Ramona would say I was out of order, but you've got to make the most of such chances in this bad weather. That copper might've thought himself high and almighty when he whacked on them cuffs but like I said, his daughter will be wanting a wedding disco come a couple of years, and she'll need to know where to go.

'Don't you be going to Johnny Discs,' I warned him. 'He anna got the vinyl like me. And he charges double and a minicab if you go past two.'

'I'll bear it in mind, Alvie,' he said. 'But she's only sixteen, remember.'

'So was mine,' I said. 'And it would've been proper nice to have walked her down the aisle.'

It was three years ago when I woke up in a filthy mood and couldn't put my finger on why. I felt like I needed to tell someone something, you know? And I'd been writing to Tony, I'd taught myself, like, and I was only telling him how disappointed I was. Oh, I know he rolled up his sleeves and went out without a tie, but that doesn't mean he's one of us, that he understands what it's been like. Like I said to him, it's like you've put an elastic band around the north and squeezed out its lifeblood. We're choking, Tony, I wrote. And we've run out of ideas.

You see it's no good when a class stops working. Hanging around in back kitchens, looking out of us windows, the wife shouting to shift the wardrobe so she could get to them skirtings—you're as low as you can be when you're on all fours with a cloth and a bowl of bleach. So I had a think while I was down there. What could I do? Who could I be now? Otherwise that's it, isn't it? Been somebody once, now a nobody with a Hoover in his hand. I said to the wife before she left, 'Either you take that bloody Hoover with you or you let me burn it,' but that's the thing when you're grieving on your own. Makes you do things you never thought your fists were capable of. But I would've loved a reply off Tony. House of Commons paper and that little gatehouse—would've really meant something to me that—stuck two fingers up at the old man at least.

So I wrote to his son. He seemed like a good lad and I wanted to thank him. Because if it wasn't for him, I wouldn't have heard my calling. And it was a little goldmine for a while. Made a bit on the side with what I could under the decks and I know our Ramona was looking down at me shaking her head, but like I told her: it's a world of entrepreneurs now. You've got to branch out. And that Johnny Discs, he was cleaning up with his compilation CDs and duty free. So I looked around the house at what I could sell and I thought, I won't sell my vinyl, no I won't. Not when every record was bought with an honest week's work. It was tradition that—every Saturday, like a fag and a pint come Friday. Symbolised a hard grafter that, deserving it was, and I'd play it to death. So I told our Ramona. I'll make those records my job. Everyone loves a party. Then came that ban. And it did more than help the country's health.

Dear Euan, I wrote. We've all been drunk. Drunk because of love or drinking away the future, it's all the same, and as for disorder, well. How do you order this many people? I said to our Ramona, it's the dawning of a new decade and the sun is shining. Bit of fags and booze at his age, it's to be expected. So I wrote to him: Come on Euan, do us a favour, eh? You're one of us now mate, back on the streets with the rest of us, and you're what, twenty-five now? Quarter of a century my son, you're a lucky blighter. Mine never knew what it was like to pass big exams and become somebody else. While you were out there throwing up a new future, my daughter was in the garage dangling, the Hoover cable around her neck.

The wife had wanted to call her Sheila, but like I said, that's no name for who she's going to be. I had to change my name. No good being an every John like everyone else. I want her knowing who she is from the off, because God, I had plans for my little girl. I'd made some real plans I had. Like I said to Euan—me and you mate have a bit of common ground. We've all known what it's like to have a disappointing dad.

Love, Alvin and Ramona.

Dear Euan, I wrote. I was like you son, the eldest of four and there's some responsibility in that. I weren't so lucky in getting a decent brood to watch over, but what I lacked in family members I had in decent mates. Course, you know who your friends are in times of redundancy. It's a bit of shock when they stop calling in for a brew. Makes you wonder what you ever had in common. But never mind eh? Bit of solitude has its moments and you get gen and make do. Story of my life that. But our Ramona, she was writing and writing. It's why I started learning. I thought there isn't any point in me sitting here and just watching her with all them pens and filling out my forms. Like I wrote to Tony, don't be judging my handwriting mate. It's not how it looks, it's what it says. People today, they take a pen for granted.

'What's up with yer?' our Ramona said, and I had to say to her, 'I don't know if I'm right or left.' And she said, 'Just go with the flow, Dad. See which feels most right.'

Course, it was stuck in me head then, but so was being left, and I can't tell you how much that got me down at first. Right-handed Alvie, I thought to myself. Never thought I'd see myself with a pen in my right hand. My father will be turning in his grave. Course, like I said to Tony. It weren't the fags but the job that killed him. It's why I never added dust to my stage name. All that dust on my father's lungs, strikes a nerve that. Not a penny in compensation.

Dear Euan, I wrote right-handed. Sorry to bug you again mate, but I'm starting to feel a bit cheated. This ban like, I don't think your dad's thought it through—because an empty ashtray is an empty pub. And an empty pub means they're all at home putting their own records on. And if they're putting their records on then they're having a party. And if they're having a party at home then there's no need to go out. Do you see what I'm getting at, Euan? Because a fuller factory makes a better place to live, and a fuller ashtray means I've got a wage. So I'm making a point here. Them buckets of sand for the butts and the dimps, that's what your old fella's doing to us lot. He's burying us in daft laws and yet his head's in the sand.

Love, Alvin and Ramona.

The wife used to say that all she ever wanted was a bay window. If you had a bay window you had a semi. And if you had a semi you had a better view. Oh, she kept a decent house and she weren't that bad a wife when she wasn't wanting. We'd be sat at the table doing us writing, me and our Ramona, and there the wife would be sat, staring out of the window. 'They've had a new car at number 6,' she'd bleat. 'They only decorated last week, and those kids are all in new uniforms. Blazers an' everything.'

And our Ramona, she'd be chewing her pen, I can see her now, and she'd tell her mother, 'Only swots have blazers.'

'Yes, I live on the wrong side of the bloody road,' the wife would say. But I could picture her in mind as the wife pictured fresh wallpaper, and so I put a bit aside and got her one.

'Oh Alvie,' said the wife. 'What are you trying to do to her?'

I used to watch her take it off when the bus came, see her coming out of school with it screwed up in her bag. Like I wrote to Tony, I agree with you mate. Sometimes you don't succeed, do you? You just don't know what it feels like knowing you're the new future. Shame though. The wife wanted to give it to the social but like I said to her: I've paid in my taxes for thirty odd years, asked no one for nothing and lived off hand-me-downs all my life. That blazer stays where she left it.

Dear Euan, I wrote, and my letters were in double figures by now. Treat it like learning to tie your own shoelaces. He's your dad. You must have a chat now and then, have a view, make a point, put the world to right, isn't that his job? Mind you, farting about in other countries, he's forgotten about the world back home. So tell him this while you're at it, Euan. Because shoelaces, son, are what family was to this country. They tie us all together, and it's the same process whether on the left or the right. Course, our Ramona was all heels by then; another six inches and she would've touched the garage floor and saved her life. I told her the night before, it won't matter a jot what letters your exam results come in. You're Ramona Starr. But what can you do, eh Euan? Ten years ago, I wouldn't even have recognised the word fail. But that's what I've found when you properly start learning. You see the word and then you see what other people think of it. And you know what the worst thing is, Euan? When you wish you hadn't bloody learnt. When you wish you couldn't read her words. Because if I hadn't learnt, I wouldn't have been able to read, 'Sorry Dad, but that's me done.'

Love, Alvin and Ramona.

Dear Euan, I wrote. What do you think about this then? Friday night in the Six Bells was my night. It was all I had left. Fifty quid, and I'd made sure it was damn right. I'd start around nine-ish, bit of Bowie to ease them in, jig things up around midnight, keep the ladies happy with some Abba. Then the old bloody landlord keeled over in the cellar. Brewery sent some young things in and gutted it. Like a bloody kitchen with all that stainless steel around. Menus for God's sake, cups and saucers and servi-bloody-ettes! I sit in here every day I do, nowt better on other than to sit here staring at my face in the stainless bloody steel and striking matches for fags I can't smoke. Like I keep saying, it was a proper pub was this. This bar was propped up—Grafters, people, pint and a fag every Friday, a little bop and a bag of cheese and onion. Because it's a bigger picture up here, Euan, I wrote, and it's clogging up my veins, because look in that stainless steel bar, Euan. Don't see a single working man's face in that bar, do you? I'm sat by myself, wanting work, bit of company, and all them lot are sat at home with a special bloody offer from Tesco and playing 'Now that's what I call fuck off' for the wife.

Love, Alvin and Ramona.

Dear Euan, I wrote for the last time. Just so you know son, that bar burnt down and another John bites the dust. It's been a pleasure mate.

Love, Alvin and Ramona.

Drive

[in 17 meanings]

#1

Whilst she drives, your mother whimpers. She isn't drunk but she has been drinking. Your father is wearing his pyjamas and it is all very normal until your mother hits the back-end of a transit and shunts the car onto the other side of the road.

—Christ! Buckle him in! Buckle him in!

You watch your father lurch towards the dash.

—Help me, Juke. Buckle him in!

But there's blood. More blood. This time from his nose. It isn't as thick as the other blood, the blood that's pooled about his kidneys, and it isn't as red either. You think this is strange.

You didn't know that you could bleed different colours from different parts of your body.

—Juke! For crying out loud! Will you buckle him in?

You can see that your mother's left arm is blotted with your father's blood and you hope it leaves a stain. She's been careless. She's making mistakes already. If it were up to you, you would've called Moth. He wouldn't have believed you at first. He'd have said—Shit, man? For real? And you'd have said—Yeah man. Like the woman is da-*ranged*. And he'd have sent round his people and you would've seen how it's done properly. But now your mother's swerving to avoid something in the middle of the road. A bollard? A traffic cone? You sway about in the back seat. No. It's roadkill. Just roadkill. A fox. You think it's a fox anyway. Animals dead on the road in the dark all look the same. And when you look behind you, in the rear window, you see there's blood on the road. Not much. But enough to assure you that the fox is dead.

#2

The car you are in is a blood-red three-door Volkswagen Polo with no four-wheel drive doing 80 mph in a 30 zone. It's not very well looked after and it's not a getaway car either. The windows are dirty and there's no water in the tank. There's barely any petrol and no one has checked the oil. This is the only car your parents own. It makes small journeys here and there and it is, like you, fifteen years old. Your mother learnt to drive in this car. Hang around long enough and so will you. She says it again:

—Juke, please! Buckle him in!

You notice that there's your father's blood under your fingernails. You don't know how it got there. You didn't put him in the car.

#3

You were standing by the car with your hood up when your mother shouted at you to drive. She was carrying your father out of the house as if carting off a pig to the slaughter. His feet were dragging on the ground and blunting his toes. You had to remind your mother that you were fifteen years old and did not have a licence. She reminded you that it hadn't bothered you before—*joy driver* she called you—and to get in the fucking car and drive. You do not enjoy your mother's temper, so you'd folded your arms and said no. You drive. And you'd got into the back of the car.

#4

Your mother stalls the car right in front of the Jet King Drive Thru Car Wash. You've robbed this place once or twice because you know where the idiot who owns the place keeps the keys. It's bought you fags. Cans. *Call of Duty* 4. You stopped robbing it in the end because it was too easy. As your mother stalls, the glovebox shoots open. Most of what was in the glovebox is now on your father's lap. Headphones, tissues, cough sweets, road map, fags, fag-butts. That means one of them is smoking again which means one of them will have driven the other one to it.

You say—You're not really going to dump him here, are you?—and you need to get your mother to drive.

—Drive! you shout. Drive!

But your mother is busy smoking a cigarette and telling your father that this is all his fault.

#5

You think about your mother while she smokes her cigarette. She is forty-four years old but could pass for someone thirty and this, you want to remind her, is exactly what she wants. She has crayon-brown eyes and copper-dyed hair that sticks to her cheeks when she cries—hair and tears are like paper and glue—and you are fascinated by the baby size of her feet, how her fingers look as if they should be served up in soup, how when she meets your friends she sucks upon strands of that copper-dyed hair and asks them—Are you cruel to your mothers too?

Because your mother speaks of everything in plurals. Still brings rude words to the table and asks you what they mean. She was driven here by plane sixteen years ago when she was part of a beauty crew serving red or white, chicken or beef, yet spent a long time calming down the man in Seat 36 Row D as he blew into a paper bag and asked if she might be kind enough to hold his hand.

Your father said he was smitten within seconds of her flushing his sick into the sky. He swears on his life that he was out there on conference, back in the day when your father *was* the conference, but you're not sure about this and neither is Moth. He has told you why men go to Asia and Moth snots on his sleeve and says you have to take him there man, cos you got family there, right? Breakfast and a lot of fucking bed. And you laugh at that because that's a joke, right? And Moth is the man with his thick fists and inked neck that's saving you from being laughed at for having hair that's as long as a girl's.

But you're still their product—from when your mother met your sick old man in the sky: they did the nasty and out came you. But different don't work round here, different don't fit. So you got to stick to the plan, man. See it through.

Connect 4. You remember how your mum and dad used to play endless games of Connect 4.

#6

Your mother has cleaned at the university for as long as you can remember and remains there by the skin of her teeth. Because everyone knows she took those papers and gave them to you so you'd know all the answers and pass the exam. But no one knows this for sure because there's not enough proof and no CCTV. So your mother goes to work and comes back even later and when your father asks her where she's been all this time she glares at you both with those crayon-brown eyes and uses some words she has learnt at her class.

—Culprits, she says. You culpables. You criminals.

And more words like—You're driving me up the wall, Juke. You're driving me round the *bluddy* bend.

But you know that your mother's drive to be an English is what's driven your father away and that your father hasn't really gone any further than his computer drive. That when you went to look at the emails again, the pictures and the messages from Bangkok weren't there. Your father had deleted everything but you were still the talk of the town.

#7

Your father quit the university to set up the Jet King Drive Thru Car Wash because he was sick of the demands, the need to publish unnecessary work. This has outraged your mother, driven her mad with shame. Yet your father has never looked happier. He is two stone less, he smiles and he laughs, asks you about the football scores, wears trainers instead of smart shoes.

You tell this to Moth. Your dad's alright, you say, but my mum, she's like *da*-ranged. You're sat on your bed with your Xbox in your room with its lemon punch walls and Moth tells you that you're going to need to learn to drive. You get nothing in this life on foot, he says. So he's got a challenge, right? Got to engineer a situ-*a-shon*. And it's something only you can do for him. Then he gets up from your bed and rips the Xbox leads from the socket. It's his now, he says. *Collateral*. And that you sleep in a little kid's room. Fucking chink baby with golden hair.

—I'm Thai, you correct.

—You're all the same to me, *he* corrects. And he punches you anyway and busts your lip.

#8

You remember the first time you met Moth. He came and called for you one night but you didn't see who was calling and you didn't see the fist either. But it connected and it hurt and you staggered and dropped to the floor. That's when someone else's hand grabbed you by your hair and dragged you out into the backyard where your jawbone slammed against concrete. You remember it smelt of petrol and dead matches down there and that the bloodstain that appeared on the paving slab is not dissimilar to the bloodstain your father now has pooled about his kidneys. You remember the blows to the ribs (sixteen), the bruised cheek, the black eye, and everything else that happened or might not have happened as you curled up into a ball on your parents' patio where they sometimes came out to smoke and argue and slug down wine.

Except that night you were all on your own. Your mother was at the university. Your father, you have no idea. But what you remember most is the way Moth spat in your face and then smeared it into your thin little eyes. Look at me or I'll rip your fucking head off chink-boy. You don't remember what you said. Probably that you were Thai. But after you'd took the beating and they'd taken all that you had, Moth sat on your shins and got out his penknife. And while you thought of your next-door neighbour's black Mini Sport with its two exhausts and sixth gear, Moth carved his name into your arm.

—Now you're in, he said, and you'd felt chuffed to bits.

The next morning you buried your head in the pillow and told your mother you were sick. She did not look at your face for two days. Then when she did she said—I knew you were too good for that school—and she and your father argued about sending you private and preferably, said your mother, to board.

You have never shown your mother or your father your arm. You wear long sleeves always. But penknives don't scar like Moth thinks. And he doesn't spell very well either. He says you had to go through that—like an initi-*ation* man—and everyone who's in goes through it too. When he introduces you to a few of his people it's what you talk about and you compare scars like boxers, warriors, vigilantes of the night. You talk about guns too, bows and arrows, of knives and knuckledusters and samurai swords. And what you're made of, what's driven you to do what you're going to do. You talk about that a lot.

#9

Some time ago your mother replaced your father with her computer. Even when your school wrote her that first letter to tell her they hadn't seen you in two weeks, and even when they called her up at work and asked her to come in because it'd been over a month since you'd attended, she still carried on typing her words. When the police found you roughing up that kid for his trainers and you got chucked in a cell for two hours and they gave you a bowl of something that looked like dog-meat, your mother just shook her head and bailed you out and told you not to get a girl pregnant like English man do before she carried on typing her words. And when you did bring a girl home and buried yourself inside of her with your socks still on, you took your bed sheets into your mother's study and left them on her desk for her to see. Even then, she washed the sheets and ironed them dry and said nothing about the blood specks and the semen and the mascara that was all over your pillows. So you stole the car you'd had your eye on from over the road—an Audi TT, three door, black leather heated seats—and you drove it up the Roaches where you torched it with Moth, and all the while it burned, you thought of your mother and that sign that hangs above her computer that says,

当你可以开车的时候, 为什么走路
Why walk when you can drive

So when you got back home—when it was past two in the morning and she was still on her computer—you'd flung open her door and shouted—fuck you for ever—and meant it, because you felt like you should never have been born.

You had no idea what she was writing. You often wish you still don't. Your father pleads with her not to publish those words—it is breaking him, he says, tearing us apart—but she does, every day. She cleans up the university then blogs all about you and it's made you the talk of the town. She has warned you that you can't stop her:

—Take my computer, I go cafés. I find ways to get to my friends—because your mother talks in viral now. She is famous because of you.

—He's Triad, is what people even think.

#10

When you look out of the car window, you realise that you're moving again and that your mother is not going to dump your father in the Portakabin at the Jet King Drive Thru Car Wash, though you can tell by her face that she'd thought about it. You know how much your mother detests the Jet King Drive Thru Car Wash because she did not run away to England to be the wife of a man who washes other people's cars. And she reminds your father how she left a man of no worth and drive back in Hong Kong. Though now he is successful businessman. Export. Import. Made in China.

—He still wants me, your mother goads. Leave all his family for me. But your father ignores her because he's still passed out.

If your father could speak he would tell her about the necessity for waxing the bonnet after rain, about the things he finds in other people's car boots when he valets. You are reminded of the time he came home and told you he'd found three dead cats in the boot of a silver Astra. All Siamese. Your mother raged at him—What are you driving at, Joel? What is your point? And he said nothing. There were just three dead cats in the boot of a silver Astra. All Siamese. That's all.

#11

Your mother is driving very fast for someone who's banned. You remember when she got banned because when the police came to the door she instantly assumed it was because of you and she told them to take you away. —Teach him a lesson, she said. Throw away the key. I am done with him. He is not my son.

He was a pig with an upturned nose and a bottle-shaped face and cigarette smoke lingered on his clothes. He looked unhappy you thought, like he'd had enough of it all too, and he asked your mother to step outside and breathe into the pipe. She'd been on the vodka most of the morning. She had that desperate look in her eyes that you see far too often for someone of your age. Like she wants you to look after her. But you don't. It's not your job. So she drinks her vodka and types her words and still gets into a car every day to drive you to school. It's the only time you ever get any time with her and even then you don't say a word because she doesn't talk to you either. She just drives. The only thing you like about that journey is that it's just you two in the car and she sometimes jumps the lights.

#12

You have still not asked your mother where you are going but this is definitely not the route to the hospital. She shouts at you:

—When we there you say nothing, you hear?

And then, because you don't answer her:

—I mean it, Juke. You don't breathe any words.

But this is fine by you because you can't remember if it was you fighting the knife off your mother or your mother fighting the knife off you or if you'd gone into their bedroom because they were fighting and if you took the knife in with you to give to her, to give to him, just that you know that the knife had tomato ketchup on it because you'd been making a crisp sandwich at the time.

#13

Your mother has stopped the car on your aunt's tarmac drive. Your mother has not thought this through. Your father needs a hospital. Accident and Emergency. Doctors expert in knife wounds. Your aunt is married to a GP who prescribes painkillers and feels your glands. Your mother is involving family and that is no good. Moth has told you that. Family can't help but tell. You get me chink-boy? And you nod at Moth and do that thing you have to do with your fist and draw blood. Then you tell him again that you're Thai.

#14

Your mother is still in the driver's seat. She has twisted her body to the left so she can look at your father. You wonder what she thinks of him right now, if this has made anything change. His chin is set deep into his neck and the blood, which has started to smell, has leaked into the car. You notice that your mother is muttering at him—you can't hear what exactly—but you know that's she's getting her story straight. Your mother is all about the words and how they appear in straight lines. She'd much rather her words than him. And even you. When you listen closely, your mother is speaking in a dialect you don't understand. You cannot Google that.

You see that your mother is wearing her dark blue knee-length T-shirt that she wears when typing her blogs that she posts out to the world about the son she cannot love. That the bloodstains, in this light, could easily be mistaken for sweat. That she'd recently cut off her hair and had threads of copper put through which would, if there'd been a moon, have glimmered. That you were making a sandwich when you heard them arguing.

He called her a drunk.

She called him an old bore.

The other said you've driven me to it while the other said no. You drove me.

He said he was fed up of wringing her out.

She said go wash your stupid cars and wring them out.

I will, he said.

For good, she said. And take him with you. I am done with the pleasings. I am done with this shammy.

And your father had laughed like a drain.

But you know your mother drove your father to it. It's not like these things don't happen. As you know exactly why your mother has driven here. Not because her sister was married to a GP, but because her sister was welcome to him.

#15

Your father has been bleeding for thirty-six minutes. He is wounded, no two ways about it, but you know that the wound is not huge because the knife wasn't driven in that far if it went in at all because the knife was blunt. His unconsciousness, therefore, is not because he is in the middle of bleeding to death, but because he is a wuss when it comes to the sight of blood. Still, thirty-six minutes of blood loss is not ideal.

—You go in, Juke. You tell them. They believes in you.

Your mother is talking to you, Juke.

—Please, Juke. Go in there and tell them what happened.

You don't know your mother's sister because you've been told to keep away. You are uncontrollable. A lout. A thug with a reputation for being duff meat. Your aunt is smart. And rich. And married to a GP who plays golf and tennis and talks of backhand drives and slicing drives out of bounds and shows you how with his hands. That was the last time you saw him at any rate and you thought him smug. So when Moth asked if you had any ideas to bring to the table to prove you were worth more than a set of robbed exam papers, that it was worth him letting the foreigner in, you told him about the smug GP and your smart rich aunt but you forgot about the CCTV. And no matter how hard you tried, none of your stones were thrown high enough to smash the lens. You throw like a girl, man. You should stick to washing cars, like your old fucking man. And that's when it occurs to you that your father *is* old. Older than you ever have thought and he's not going to be around for ever.

So you say to your mum —Did you marry him for his money or a visa?

Your mother looks at you in the rear view mirror and says —Both.

And me? you say. What the fuck about me?

Your mother smiles. —I don't know. Juke. What the fuck about you?

—You made me! you shout. You and him. You made me!

—And you scares me! she shouts back. I look for help. Someone who know what to do. Your father say 'Ignore him! He just growing!'—and she punches your father then for his uselessness, his lack of everything, for telling her nothing about English life, and she says it again:

—Please, Juke. You tell them it was accident. They believe you like I believes you.

And she cries and asks for your hands. You give them to her. Not because you're a sop but because you can't be arsed arguing with her any more. You are done even if she's not, and she takes both your hands in hers and kisses them sloppily. By the time she has done with you, your hands are damp with her saliva, his blood. Or her blood, his saliva. You have now forgotten who stabbed who.

—Please, Jukey. Go tell them what happened. How it was accident.

You pull away your hands at that. Not because your mother is lying, but because you hate who you are and blame her. So you tell her again how you're ribbed for your stupid name, your flowing blonde hair and Asian eyes; your wiry little body neither black, brown nor white that won't grow up, grow out, or do what normal bodies do. How you get taunted:

—Is that your Grandad?

—Does your mum give good head for ten dollar?

How all you really want is a mum and a dad like everyone else. So stop it with the fucking Jukey and pretending this is all OK. This is not OK. You and him have never been OK.

—Now you listen, she starts. Love is a bluddy funny thing and you is our son Juke. I just wish—but she runs out of words and speaks to you in Thai. So you give her some of yours.

—Careful what you fucking wish for, eh? Because you know it wasn't ever for you.

#16

You look out of the window at your aunt's house. You don't know what she does or why she has so much money or when she came to England and if her coming to England and having all of this is what drove your mum to come on the plane and pretend she was the stewardess—red or white, chicken or beef—because your aunt knew the pilot and the pilot said —For Favour— and if her sister could do it so could she.

Moth keeps asking about your aunt. She on my rad-*arrr*, he says. What your family has out there is worth fucking gold, man—and he wants an in. But you can't give him an in on a field full of cows and house covered in CCTV.

—Moth man, you say. It's just a fucking farm. A drive of cattle in a field.

—But they've got guns, man, says Moth. With licence. With poss-*i-bil-ity*.

And he wants you to get him a gun from the farm. Moth wants a gun. He has always wanted a gun. And you're the only one who can get him one which makes you superi-*ahh*.

—I'm talking the front seat man, says Moth, with his right hand on your back and his left about your throat. And like a moth to a flame you agree.

While you're thinking about all of this, your mother starts talking again. She says:

—I have no ideas what drives you, what drives him, why I drove us all here, but I did and I'm out of ideas—and she gets out of the car to go knock on the door.

#17

You wonder if now is the time to get the gun. You got your distraction. It all went to plan and everyone'll be busy with your father when they find him. No one will miss you. You could get one and stash it in the boot and cover it over with that big blanket you brought with you. The one you told your mother would keep your father warm in blood loss. Then you could drive away.

You think about getting into the driver's seat instead and just driving off. You could go anywhere. Just drive until the tank runs dry. You think about what to do with your old man. Except your father has begun to wake and it takes you by surprise. He lurches forward as if he's just remembered how to breathe again and he brings up his hands to his face and sees the blood. —Oh my God he says and he sucks in his belly, looks down and starts to wail like a small child wanting chocolate. You tell him to man up and get a grip. It was only the blunt butter knife and he'd been cheating on his wife with her sister.

—Anyway, you say. It's probably only tomato ketchup because you were making a crisp sandwich at the time.

So you tell him where you are to reassure him then get out of the car and go see if you can get your gun.

The Trees in the Wood

IT'S NOT THAT I don't sleep. I know I don't *not* sleep. I could fall asleep right now if I wanted to, but that's not what they want me to do. And Mia was fine about it when I asked her, if not a little distracted. But then she's always distracted by something. Her mobile phone rings all the time, then there's the home phone and now her pager. 'It's just that I don't remember giving you my number,' she'd said when I called her again to confirm. And she still looks confused when she opens the door to me today.

'What are you bringing me now?' she says, pointing to my overnight bag. I try and distract her with my usual offering of wine. She says, 'Laura, what do I keep saying about bringing me wine?' But she still tucks the bottle under her arm, I could see she'd already got a glass on the go, and the bag gets forgotten because then her mobile goes. It's her friend Liz and she's told quickly, 'Not really. Laura's here. It's Tuesday, isn't it?' And it sounds so very unkind.

But then she was all apologies: it was just pasta and pesto for tea because she'd not got to the supermarket and she was sure that's what she'd given me last week, which she did, but I didn't tell her so. Besides, it was all the twins would eat. And then her mobile goes again and she sighs but when she looks at the number she's smiling. She sticks her head in the fridge to answer it, as if looking for the milk which is already on the side, and her voice is muffled, low, but sweet. 'Hi,' she says, and, 'No, not really, but I can later. Yeah, I'd like that too.' And then she shuts the fridge and says, 'Actually tonight is difficult. It's Tuesday, isn't it?' And I see that she's not washed yesterday's plates, that the breakfast bowls are still on the table, that they seem to have acquired a cat because what's down there on the floor by the patio door looks like a bowl of its food.

'Right, drink,' and Mia's back in the kitchen, her mobile back in her pocket, and she's still in her nurse's uniform after a twelve-hour shift with her silver grizzled hair tied into a too-tight ponytail that sucks up her face. She fills the kettle, fills her glass and starts to swill out a mug for me. She talks with her back to me, asks, 'What's new with you?' and then before I can speak she turns and says, 'Oh my goodness! Did I tell you Rowan made Oxford?' and because she suddenly looks so happy I'm forced to smile and say, 'No.'

Rowan is Mia's eldest daughter and brilliant at science, chemistry's her thing, and though this is good, that Rowan will finally be moving out—their relationship is a little fraught to say the least—Mia covers her face with her hands and mutters something about the first from the nest and what will she do without her? I want to say, 'Plenty,' but the hands are removed and she suddenly shouts, 'Oh my God, did I tell you my mother was attacked?'

I look startled. 'No,' I say, and would rather not hear any more, as I'm sure Mia, if she was thinking straight, wouldn't tell me either given how much she knows I detest the night, but she does and she says, 'Do you know what the worst part is? I'm glad. I'm actually really fucking glad because now I can do what I should've done years back.' And I wish she wouldn't swear because she sounds bitter and cantankerous and she knows I don't like it. But then the home phone starts up and she's hunting it down and I see it flashing beside a pile of magazines on the seat of the armchair she keeps in the kitchen by the range which she had fitted almost two years ago and still doesn't know how to use.

Nor does she know how to use the home phone either, because when she answers it's on speakerphone so I get to hear: 'Mrs Onions? Edith Davenport. Davenport House. Just to say that the room is now ready for you and we can send a removal team for a week Friday. Does that give your mother enough time?' And I can see that Mia's panicking about me hearing this because she tells this Edith Davenport to hang on, she's on speakerphone and she doesn't know which button it is to get it off. Edith Davenport laughs and says, 'Technology, eh?' and Mia agrees: technology will be the death of her if lack of sleep doesn't get to her first. And I raise my eyebrows at this and glare because she can't have forgotten why I am here.

Eventually, she asks Edith Davenport to call her on her mobile. 'Because if I didn't know how to use that I'd never speak to my eldest daughter at all,' and she sounds so very sad when she says it. So the call ends and she suddenly remembers I'm here and goes, 'Laura. Shit. Drink. At least let me get you a drink. Things aren't normally like this.' I tell her, 'Actually, Mia, they are.' She gives me the sort of look that makes me feel unwashed, except her mobile is ringing. She says, 'I'm not sure there's teabags but there's coffee so help yourself. You know where everything is,' and goes into the hallway to answer her phone.

This leaves me in the kitchen with the twins, Margot and Henry, who have just turned five and are still in their school uniforms squabbling over jigsaw pieces under the kitchen table where they now also like to eat. I have told Mia that I don't agree with them eating off the floor like dogs, but she says at least they're eating and it keeps them quiet and I spot a few rubbery-looking pasta twirls on the floor and a dollop of what looks like hardened ketchup.

I look down at the jigsaw. 'I like a jigsaw,' I tell the twins. 'A doctor, though I use the word lightly, once prescribed me a jigsaw with a nip of whisky each night, and diagnosed me as still not grieving as if that were an actual medical term then sent me to a counsellor who never spoke. "I'm not the subject Laura, you are," he said to me. So we talked about the art on his walls and his mother's dementia and I tried to have him struck off but apparently depression is now two a penny and there's not enough counsellors to go round.'

I pick up a couple of pieces of the jigsaw and start to fit them together on the floor. Margot frowns at me. 'We were doing that,' she tells me. 'We don't need your help.'

'Of course you do,' I say, smiling. 'You need to get the four corners in place which helps you to work on the edges, see? *Then* you fill in the main picture.' I show them what I mean and as I do, I think about what Mia said to me when I told her about the counsellor. How she asked for my pills and looked them up in her medical journal and told me to throw them away. 'I'll help you,' she said to me, and promised to speak to a doctor she knew, but what he said and if she did is something I still don't know.

'That was two years ago,' I tell the twins. 'And I've been on at least six different medications since then, none of which have worked, and now I'm with this new doctor and on this new medication which can't be right because I'm not sleeping at all now, not a wink, and the pills are this funny shape.'

I see that Henry has collected up the rest of the jigsaw pieces and put them behind his back. I ask him what he's doing. He asks *me* what I'm doing here. 'I'm here because this new doctor has prescribed enforced wakefulness and told me to be wakeful with someone I trust not sleepless alone,' I say crossly. Though the doctor has warned me it could be short-lived. 'Short-lived positivity,' is what he said. 'That could be lost once you sleep again but at least you will have felt something else that could become the flicker of light in the next darkness.' It had sounded so beautiful I actually cried.

I look down at the jigsaw again. 'You're doing it the hard way,' I tell the twins. 'You're far better off getting your edges in place.' But Henry pulls all the pieces apart and throws them about. I put it down to not enough attention. He's normally such a docile little boy.

I open the drawer that I thought had spoons but find a pile of official-looking documents and a plane ticket for the passenger Ms Mia Richer. So I look at one of the letters, it's hard not to see their contents really, and see that she has changed her name from Mrs Mia Onions and accepted a position at a hospital in Christchurch, New Zealand, who are expecting her in February but will forward the files before, and suddenly everything stops and I can't breathe.

I manage to shut the drawer as Mia comes back into the kitchen shouting, 'Right. Pasta!' and just make out her ordering the twins to go and wash their hands because clean hands means ice cream. Then she places a hand on my shoulder and says, 'What am I like, Laura? It's almost six o'clock and I've not even asked how you are. Is this new doctor being a help?' And though I am smiling—I must be because I feel my lip muscles stretch—the words 'I'm dying, Mia' still drop from my mouth and onto the floor like weights.

But she's too distracted to notice, too flustered about the tea, and she moves from my side to scrub at a pan and starts to tell me that she's got her mother a room in a sheltered accommodation place because this cannot go on and she'll at least know where she is and what she's been doing, because if I remember this rightly her mother, though eighty, still likes a drink. And as Mia scrubs at the pan, which I feel down my thighs, it comes out again, 'For Christ's sake, Mia, I'm dying,' only this time I've yelled every word.

She drops the pan and starts rummaging in a drawer. She pulls out what looks like a Hoover bag. 'It'll have to do,' she says, which means it is a Hoover bag, and she holds it up to my face and tells me to breathe—*in, out, calm, that's it*—like she does, in that voice, one hand in my hand and the other reaching for kitchen towel which she dampens in the pan she's been scrubbing and places along the back of my neck. She says, 'There are no wasps Laura, only me,' because I've started to swat, and she grabs at my hand and squeezes it so tight I yelp. I yell into the bag, 'Don't leave me! Don't ever leave me!' and she tells me to *Sshh!*

'It's all OK, Laura. I'm here.'

She leads me to the armchair and chucks the magazines onto the floor where they will remain, I'm sure, until next Tuesday, when I come again, and she helps me sit and tells me to keep breathing into the Hoover bag. She fetches me a glass of water and says she's got to get the pasta on for the kids, and even though she's only three feet away from me, on the other side of the kitchen, she is already on the other side of the world.

As I breathe, I hear pasta rattle into a barely scrubbed pan, the kettle boiling again, the clink of jars and tins as she roots for pesto which she does with a glass of wine in her hand, and I see that under the table the twins have spread out tea towels like picnic blankets and are holding forks that look like they've been everywhere except the sink. While Mia drains pasta through a sieve at ten past six, she asks the twins about school: 'Henry, did you do your spellings and was it yoga today, Margot, or just gym?' Their voices swarm as Henry says he spelt tablet with an i but still got his name on the rainbow and Margot says she tumbled off the high horse and got a badge for landing with both feet. She scurries off to find the badge and Henry spells t-a-b-l-*e*-t emphasising the *e* and I call out to Mia, '*My* tablets, in my bag,' but the bowls of pasta come first with a squirt of tomato ketchup that comes out like a sneeze, and she places both bowls under the table before she looks for my bag and unzips.

'My clever kids,' Mia is saying as she roots in my bag. 'One day you'll rule the world and look after me!' Henry tells her he will buy her a swimming pool and Margot says they'll go shopping every day for sparkly shoes, and Mia is on her haunches and ruffling their hair and as they blow each other kisses her pager goes and she takes it from her pocket and sighs.

'Oh dear. He went without me.' Which means one of her patients has really died, palliative care nurse as she is at the hospice where we met, three years ago now, when I was nursing my mother, and where she'd asked for the job there to help with her own grief because grief, she had said, was a killer. All I said, after Mother finally went, was that I couldn't go home but knew nowhere else, I'd been sat at her bedside for so long.

'Come and have a meal at mine,' she'd said. 'It's only pasta. It's all the kids will eat. But I do make my own pesto.'

Which she did, back then, before the baby, before Rowan got into Oxford and when her husband was still coming home.

When I sat at this kitchen table and told her all about my mother without the phones going, the twins still in high chairs, when she listened to everything I had to say. When I told her it was in my blood, that I had stopped Mother, found Mother, had Mother put away until the death she willed came of its own accord. When after a year of Tuesdays, when I'd become too frightened to sleep, she lost her rag and yelled: 'Christ, Laura. Have my life for a day and you'll know what sleep deprivation is. Try losing a child. Have twins at forty fucking four. Work in palliative care for a dying NHS. You think I don't know depression? You think I don't understand why you don't sleep?' And then the worst bit: 'Where's your family, Laura? Why do you keep on coming here? What is it that you think I can do?'

What she can do is be wakeful with me. 'I need to be wakeful with someone I trust not sleepless alone,' I'd explained when I called her up to ask if I might stay overnight. And though she mentioned the twins—'You know they don't sleep, Laura'—mentioned Rowan and her friends—'She comes in when she wants now. I just count the shoes to know who's here'—reminded me of Paul—'He works late. He's elephant footed'—I explained that it was the kind of noises I needed. 'And you have a spare room,' I'd said. 'You won't even know I am there.' But she went quiet at this. She was quiet for a very long time. 'It's not spare,' she snapped eventually. 'But there's the armchair in the kitchen if you like.'

Mia comes from under the kitchen table and looks at the box of pills in her hand. She squints at the label, though her glasses are parked on her head, and tells me she'd rather I take one on a full stomach. Then she checks the time and checks her phone and just listens, and I realise that this is the first time she has thought about the baby since I got here. I want to say, 'He was never here, Mia. He never made it home.' But the moment isn't long enough and the spare room remains spare, and then the home phone starts up and she rushes off to answer it because it's half past six which means it's Paul.

She does what she always does: clips her voice, shuts down, reels off stock answers that are the same every week: Rowan is out. The twins are fine. There'll be cold pasta in the fridge. Yes, she's tired but Laura's here. It's Tuesday, isn't it? He offers to call later, I assume, because she says, 'Not to worry. I'm exhausted anyway. Though Laura wants to do that sleepless thing,' and I still don't know what it is that Paul does, just that he works with computers and that he's often in the States now on trips that can last all week.

I trade the Hoover bag for pasta and eat it in the armchair. Not because I can't get up to the table but because I suddenly feel so terribly defiant. I find myself saying, 'You've not asked me a single thing yet about what I'm to do tonight when I'm relying on you, Mia. I can't do this on my own.' And she sighs at me and puts down her fork.

'You know, my mother got attacked by a bunch of kids last Saturday night,' she says. 'They'd followed her home from the pub. Gold, they said. Old women always have gold. Even took the earrings from her ears. When the police call me, she's already in hospital. Stuffed in a bed in renal with a fractured ankle and bruised wrists where they'd grabbed her and dragged her about. Christ knows what they thought she had. But they took it all. And do you know what she says to me? "We've all been there, Mia. They're just kids who can't handle their drink."' She stops to drink wine then instructs Margot to eat—'No, you're not full, Margot. I can still see room in your belly'—and as Margot giggles at her mum's tickling socked foot, Mia tosses the pills in my lap.

'Right then, ice cream!' and I watch Mia chisel out ice cream as bright as cheese from a tub with a bread knife. Henry asks for sprinkles and strawberry sauce—she has neither—and Margot wants a flake and a surprise. Mia snaps a flake in half—there's only one—and roots through the cupboards again. She presents them with two bowls of too-cold ice cream with a dusting of hot chocolate, half a broken flake, a squeeze of honey, and they look at their cocktail glasses wide-eyed. There's even little cocktail umbrellas that she's found, like she finds their missing socks, time for cuddles and bedtime stories that go beyond the page, and she says, 'Go on then. But only half the film before bath. You have school.' And they skip into the other room to watch the telly. Then she turns to me sadly: 'I'm crap at this, Laura. I'm crap at it all.'

But her pager goes and she's looking down on it and the sadness is replaced with rage. She tells me that they can't move the body until morning because there's no spare porter on shift until 6 a.m. and the family are going berserk. 'I leave them for five fucking minutes,' she says, and reaches for her mobile and scrolls through the numbers, makes a call. She's snappy. 'Phone fucking Ken then! You cannot leave him there overnight.' Then she's running her hand through her hair, finds her glasses, puts them on, drinks more wine. 'I'll phone Ken then,' and she's scrolling through the numbers again, finding Ken, and this time she's sympathetic. 'I know, I know,' she says. Pause. Hmmm. 'But do it for me, please?' And he does. I don't know how she does it, but Ken is driving back to work to wheel a man who is ninety-six to the mortuary and give him the respect he deserves.

You're amazing, I think. How do you not sleep?

She puts down the phone and downs the wine. She's tired and she looks it yet she smiles at me. At my half-eaten bowl of pasta. 'You'll get ice cream if you finish that,' she says, and I find I am smiling back. I pick up the box of pills from my lap and say, 'It's the other ones I want you to look at. They're ever such a funny shape and I'm not sleeping. Not sleeping at all. I mean, I know I'm not *meant* to be sleeping tonight, and I know

I don't *not* sleep. But I don't want to be taking one of my panic pills if that's going to make me sleep when that's not what they want me to do. But when I close my eyes to sleep I fear I will never know life again.'

She runs her hand though her hair and pulls the ponytail loose. 'Laura,' she begins, and rubs at her face hard as if stopping herself from saying something other than, 'Did he give you any information that I should read before we do this?'

'Of course,' I say. 'There's a whole booklet we need to go through. I've read it myself, gone through it a couple of times and made notes. But it's the afterwards that's bothering me and what pills I should take in the morning because I'm going to be very tired but still awake. So I've bought enough clothes for forty-eight hours just in case, though I can always pop home and get more if you think I'd be better staying here, because it's not the during but the afterwards that he says could be worse...' But the home phone is going again. She throws up her hands—*I don't believe this*—as neither do I, and she leaves the room just as the answer-machine clicks in. It's Rowan. She wants picking up at nine and might have a friend with her. Mia grabs the phone.

'Rowan. No, I'm here. I didn't know you were working, why didn't you say? ... Because it's Tuesday, isn't it? Laura's here ... What? No. I can't do that, Rowan. You'll have to get a taxi.' She sighs loudly. 'Yes, yes, I'll pay him when you get here. Bye.' And then she shrieks at the twins: 'Bath! Now!' Because she's just realised that it's half past seven and she comes back into the kitchen to tell me this. 'Help yourself to whatever,' she says, though I've barely touched my pasta. 'Ice cream, wine. Now get up those stairs before I drag you up them!' And as she heads off to chase the twins up the stairs, I am left thinking of her own mother whom I've never met, not even seen a photograph of, being dragged around by a bunch of kids for her gold. It makes me look at my wrists and I check them over. I think of the pills in my hand, in my bag, those of my mother's which I swallowed one by one by one and how they didn't work, *it didn't work*, and I go to my bag and the panic surges from the back of my throat.

'Now, you *can* call,' this new doctor had said. 'If anything starts to feel wrong you must call.' And I think about using her phone. I could use her phone, couldn't I? Help yourself to whatever, she'd said. She wouldn't mind. So I do.

I don't know what makes me do it. I've watched her scroll through her numbers so many times now I know her address book off by heart. I'm surprised when he answers. 'Hello,' he says, and 'What's up?' He sounds like he's working, he's distracted anyway, and I hear him tap, tap at a computer. 'Mia?' he says. And he sounds decent. He works too much and he stays away from her and they talk on the phone as if cold calling about double glazing, but I also remember Mia once said to me, 'Either I'll have an affair, he will or we will part if I don't start dealing with it.' But they haven't parted, not yet, and he does sound decent. Like he cares. So I tell him: 'I'm a very good friend of your wife who is upstairs bathing your children at almost eight when they should be in bed. Your other daughter is coming home from work in a taxi that she cannot afford and there's a plane ticket in the kitchen drawer. She's accepted a job in New Zealand and it's time you took down that cot from the spare room. There is also someone who calls who makes her smile. I think these are things you ought to know.' I put down the phone.

It's not that I don't sleep. I know I don't *not* sleep. I could fall asleep right now if I wanted to, but that's not what they want me to do. And Mia was fine about it when I asked her, if not a little distracted, but then she's always distracted by something.

Her mobile rings all the time, then it's the home phone or her pager. Everyone wants a piece of her. Even when she's incomplete. My mother used to tear pieces off me. For wanting to work here. For taking a job there. For taking up driving lessons. For not coming home when I said. 'It makes me panic, Laura,' she would say as I'd stick my fingers down her throat. 'I don't like not knowing where you are. When you're with me, I can get out of the woods.' But she allowed those trees to keep on growing.

Mia is gone for a long time upstairs. There isn't much chatter. No arguments or messing, as she calls it. The twins are tired. They will sleep easy but waken, as they do, and crawl into her bed so that Paul will get up and sleep in the armchair beside the range that they still don't know how to use. Except Mia will stay awake. Sniffing their foreheads, stroking their cheeks, kissing them all over, just in case, just in case.

'You can't keep watching them, Mia,' I once heard Paul saying over the monitor one evening as I put on my coat to head home. 'They are not Ben. Ben was never going to last the night. We always knew that.' And Mia had wept. She'd nursed all her life, she'd said. If anyone could've saved him, it should have been her. 'I just want to sleep, Paul,' she had cried. 'I want to go to sleep and not ever wake up.'

Mia comes back into the kitchen looking weary. She is surprised to see me, as if she's forgotten I was there at all. 'I'm so sorry,' she begins, and she checks the time and fills her glass and asks if she can look at the booklet. 'But you have your coat on,' she points out.

'I do,' I say.

'You don't have to go,' she says. 'I'm more than happy to do this with you. I'll take a shower in a minute. That'll perk me up. Just let me take a look at these new pills so I know what I'm dealing with.' And she holds out her hands. But I don't give her the box. I give her my hands.

'Get some sleep, Mrs Onions,' I instruct and let myself out into the night.

As I walk down the street, a car comes hurtling around the corner as if a life depended upon it. I know it's Paul though I have met him only briefly, but it's him and it makes me glow with the sort of happiness I thought I would never know again. And then a taxi appears, struggling around the bend. Rowan will get out, run in for her mother's money, and then, perhaps, they will talk, the three of them, about Oxford, about New Zealand, about what happens next. Perhaps they will all get some sleep.

I throw all the pills I have stashed in my overnight bag into the next litter bin I see. It's not a big feeling that I have but it's a positive one and I have no idea for how long it will last. That new doctor had said, 'Be wakeful with someone you trust not sleepless alone,' though he did warn it'd be short-lived. 'Short-lived positivity,' he'd said. 'That could be lost once you sleep again but at least you will have felt something else.' Though I'd call it short lives. Mia knows that better than anyone. As I know that I need to start trusting myself that I can sleep alone. And I don't *not* sleep that night. But I do feel like I know where some of the pieces are now. And that's a jigsaw only I can complete.

Fron

It was never meant to be a vast life anyway. Small, he'd said. We'll live like dormice, fuck like rabbits. He was drafting his resignation letter at the time.

But when she arrived, and in the dark, her breath took up all the room. A cold place, grey stone, thick slate, and damp. It was the first thing she could smell. Then, that stench that comes with opening a fridge door that hasn't been used in months.

She hit the lights.

Jesus, Michael.

He was sitting at the table with a glass of wine and a bouquet of nettles wrapped in silver foil.

You took your time.

He pushed the stinging bouquet towards her.

For you.

She doesn't look at them. She knows what he wants her to say.

How long have you been here? I thought we said eight.

She is sharp with him. He is sharper with her.

Where have *you* been?

What do you mean where have *I* been?

She throws her car keys onto the table in front of him.

Leaving, Michael. It takes time to leave.

He looks at her jealously. Starts with the questions. How was it? How did he take it? Did you get lost on the way up? I told you—left turn at the crossroads, left again. You can miss it completely in the fog. Did you miss it?

Yes, she'd missed it. She'd had to go back down to come up again by which time the fog had settled in dense chunks. As she'd started back down, she had kept going. Missed the turning a second time. There were less people in the world up here than there were down there. Not enough people and you missed your way. She'd not seen a signpost in hours. It'd dropped dark and got darker.

I don't know if I can do this, Michael.

He pushes the bouquet of nettles closer. She ignores them. She is in no mood. Thinks of her mother, all of a sudden. Their last cup of tea.

No man is a good man. Her mother's words. He is just a man.

She turns around. She looks at the colour on the walls. It's the same colour as the old flannel she would bathe her mother with. An only child. So much responsibility in the end.

Wow. It really is small.

She stretches out her arms. She can touch both sides of the walls in both directions with the palm of her hands. She could, with fingers splayed, have a thumb on where she'd left and little finger on where she'd come to on the map. It'd not seemed so far on paper.

How in the hell did you bring up kids here?

We did.

When he speaks, he smokes, the air is so cold. She catches it with her hands, warms it, blows it back to him. This was not how she'd imagined it.

He is behind her now. She can feel the nettles on the back of her neck. She brushes him off.

Stop it. I've only just walked in.

She picks up a kettle, stainless steel and heavy with water.

Cup of tea?

He does not answer. He is looking for more wine.

You've been drinking all day, haven't you?

He does not answer that either.

She knows better than to ask him again.

You got what you wanted.

Perhaps. But now she's not so sure.

She finds mugs, tea-stained and dusty. Turns on the tap at the sink and runs her fingers under the water.

Is there any hot water?

The water runs cold.

Is there no hot water?

He has found wine. Red. He unscrews the cap, returns to the table to fill his glass.

No hot water at all?

She thinks about this. Then of the nettles. She will need hot water, she says. A bath, at least. He gestures towards the log burner behind him. It is heavy, black and silent; lifts an iron kettle off a stand and places it on the top.

Hot water, he says.

She sucks in her breath.

No. It's not properly sealed. I'll boil the kettle instead.

~

The kettle in the kitchen is over-boiling. She turns it off at the wall. The kitchen is full of smoke. She thinks about opening the door but she's not ready to let the outside in. She stands in the steam and closes her eyes. There is a smell, suddenly, like open flesh, and she looks down at the floor.

What's that smell?

He is at the log burner, filling it with sticks.

Can you smell it?

He strikes a match. Throws it onto the sticks.

God, what is *that* smell?

He bends down to blow on the sticks.

Can't you smell it?

He looks up from the log burner with sooty hands. She stares at his hands for so long they no longer look part of his body.

You were asked not to light it, she says. They begged you not to light it. Why didn't you do as you were told?

She goes back into the kitchen and drops two teabags into the two mugs she has swilled with cold water. She lifts the kettle. The water that comes out is brown. Black bits float in it. Like petals drooping at an unattended grave. She lifts the lid off the kettle, screams and drops it to the floor. Screams again because she is scalded. Kicks the kettle. It hits Michael in the shin.

There is something in the kettle boiled to death and the kitchen is filled with smoke.

You're on fire, she says.

Warm your hands on me, then.

But when she touches him he is so cold, her hands go right through him.

They curl up on the settee in the little front room. The open fire cackles. They drink more wine. He has forgotten about the nettles and she has scalded her foot. A dampened tea towel is wrapped around it. A blister she will have to burst come morning.

I can't believe you all actually lived here, she says. It's so *small*. It's like we've been buried into the hill.

He watches the fire.

It's all so big to a kid. We were never in anyway. We lived out there.

He rubs his mouth against the top of her head. She feels his teeth against her skin.

You smell like wet ash, she says.

She thinks of the nettles on the dining-room table and wonders if she should throw them on the fire for more warmth. Enough, she will say. Stop making me do these things. I'm here now. I'm here. I've left.

She leans forward to lift the tea towel, to check on her foot.

God, that really hurt, she says.

He examines her foot. It needs an expert's attention but the hospital is over thirty miles away. And he is drunk. And she is almost. And they are here. They are actually here.

Fron, she says. Who'd have thought that we'd end up trying to start up in Fron?

He jerks suddenly, lunges, and he's sick, violently and red in the coat scuttle. He whips the tea towel off her foot and holds it against his mouth. Vomits again. She sighs. He retches. Then she laughs. So does he.

Exactly how we met, she says.

When she wakes in the morning she is alone. His side of the bed is cold. She takes in the room. There is no daylight, and she wonders for the time. She'd counted five clocks in the house last night, all stopped at different times. Twenty past four. Quarter past eight. She lies there waiting. He will bring her coffee soon. They will make love. They will talk about how to fill the day. Ten to seven. Just after nine. They will go outside. He will show her the things he has talked about so often, the views he's created in her mind. Five to twelve. She cannot believe they are actually here. It is primitive. Way beyond. Fron.

She doesn't know if she can do this. This is *too* far away.

She needs to use the bathroom. Swings her legs out of the bed, is surprised to find she is dressed. Leggings. T-shirt. She cannot remember putting these back on. She remembers her foot, looks down and sees nothing. She sits back on the bed and lifts her foot to check again. No red mark. No blister. She listens. Looks about the room. Michael?

Silence replies.

She pads along the small landing where an electric heater ticks out a waft of warm air. She finds comfort in the heat, stands there, for a second or two, warming her feet. Then she calls him again.

Michael?

This time she questions him, like she has always done. Like he her.

Will you leave her?

Will you leave him?

There is still so much to tell each other.

I have a place, in the hills, under the sky. No one will know we are there.

Are you embarrassed of me, Michael?

No. But I do want to run away with you.

She must use the bathroom. She hovers over the toilet for the seat is icy cold. Smells the damp up above, down below. This place is awful, she thinks. Wills herself to think of it otherwise. Lives left behind. Lives started again. Living like dormice, fucking like rabbits.

Michael? Her voice is more determined.

She goes downstairs. A shaft of daylight shimmers on the carpet in front of her. Dust dances within it. She sees pictures now, on the wall, three brown-haired boys and the lone blue-eyed girl that would leave school to bear a child no one knew what to do with; all in slate-grey uniforms and drawn-on smiles. Another clock. One she had not seen last night. Twenty-five past five. Two hands entwined on the same number.

Michael?

She goes into the small living room. Finds the tea towel on the carpet but the coal scuttle is empty and scrubbed clean. She holds up the tea towel with her fingertips and can see no evidence of the night's events.

There would be no room for a child anyway. Two people is even too many.

Michael?

Afraid now. She goes into the smaller room at the back of the house. On the table, a full glass of red wine and a bouquet of nettles. There is no fire. The stone floor underneath feels made of ice. In the tiny kitchen, everything as it was, as if she had not even arrived. She looks inside the kettle with half-slit eyes and is relieved to find it empty.

He has gone to get supplies, she tells herself, filling the kettle with the cold, cold water from the tap. This was his home, where he grew up, he will have gone to knock on a neighbour, inform them of his return. She will meet them later. You and your fancy bright life, they will say. You won't last five minutes up here. She drops a teabag into a mug. Opens the fridge for the milk and it's not there. She looks down into the bag of shopping she'd brought with her last night and the two pints are not there either.

Goddamn you, Michael.

He has drunk the milk. He has gone to get milk. She goes back upstairs to shower.

~

She dresses in his clothes. Thinks about unpacking a case. She opens the wardrobe and coughs at the dust. She remembers the shopping list. Cleaning products. Freezer items. Plenty of wine. They are just three weeks into January and he has told her of harsh winters frozen in, of cracked lips and cold sores, of journeys never made. She descends the stairs as she would a hill, on the balls of her feet. Her mug of tea with the teabag still stewing waits for further instruction. Like she waits. She does not know what to do up here in Fron. How people are expected to live here when winter sets in. She pulls on her walking shoes. Thinks about her scalded foot. Removes the shoe, then the sock—it's like nothing has happened. She puts the shoes back on. Grabs her jacket and opens the kitchen door.

The fog weighs heavy. Something crows. She can barely see where she is and is afraid to go too far in case she should not find her way back. She takes small steps. That's what they will do: take small steps. Twenty years of marriage for her. His second marriage for him. She thanks God again for not giving her children. Thinks of Michael's daughter who didn't make it past four. Damage limitation, they'd called it. She was a very poorly soul. She'd watched her husband pack her cases himself and put them into the boot of her car.

That's it?

That's it. You must do what you have to do.

He even shakes her hand and thanks her for giving it a go.

She turns to look back at the cottage. She has barely gone a few metres and yet it seems like miles away. Whitewashed and desolate yet smoke pluming from the chimney. Neither fire was lit when she left. Michael must be back. She wonders when he passed her and how they'd missed each other. Just think, she would say, if you'd not looked at me as I'd looked at you. We would have missed each other. We would never have known.

She pulls her jacket tighter and heads back towards the little cottage under the hill she now cannot see for the fog.

She opens the back door and stamps her feet on a doormat as if they are caked in snow.

Michael? She blows into her hands. Michael?

In the dining room the glass of red, the nettles lying beside. In the living room, the tea towel where she'd left it on the floor. Both fires out.

Michael?

She runs back outside. It doesn't matter how far or if she can make her way back, she just needs to see, see it again from over here and sure enough, smoke, billowing now, from the chimney of the little cottage under the hill she cannot see for the fog. She runs back to the house.

Michael!

Glass of red on the table with the nettles lying beside. In the living room the tea towel where she'd left it on the floor.

Michael?

She wonders if there is another room she doesn't know about.

She wonders how six people coped with icicles as perilous as thorns.

She runs back outside and to her car, cups her hand against the window and sees only a map on the passenger seat, a blunt red line around the contours of Fron.

She runs back to the house for her keys. She will go looking for him. As he said he would look for her. Because this is it now, this is *us*.

He is hiding her away.

She finds her handbag and finds her keys, runs back to the car. She starts to drive. The fog is everywhere and everywhere there is fog, but she can just make out the lane straight ahead. She's afraid to blink. She wipes her nose, is astonished to find she is crying, and punches the glovebox open to find tissues. She drives and she drives and feels the lane lowering, as if she is sinking, as if the world below is devouring her. She puts her foot down. She can see more clearly now and yes, there is the grey pencil line of the sea; the darker blunter pencil that colours in the sky. Doll-white cottages dotted here, dotted there. Like a world without sides up here. Hell up high. She curses him.

Fuck you, Michael. You wanted this. *You* wanted this. They were just looks, Michael. Nosy parkers and blabbermouths. We would have survived.

And drives faster, looking for life.

A house on the roadside. She runs to it, hammers on the door. A shadow forms, in the frosted glass, a key is turned. A man, old and hunched in holed clothes and slippers.

Michael, she spits. Michael Connolly. Have you seen him?

The old man cups a hand around his ear.

Michael Connolly, she shouts. From Fron. Have you seen him?

The old man says something, holds out his hands. She says his name again—Michael Connolly—and points to the sky around her—from Fron, *Fron*—and the old man looks concerned, says something she cannot understand. He is Welsh. She cannot speak Welsh, doesn't understand Welsh. She throws her hands over her head and runs back to the car. When she looks back the door has been closed and the old man has gone. Like he too was never there.

She drives further down the lane that feels far longer than how it felt last night when she'd arrived. When she'd driven, heart in mouth, map on seat, a red line circling the word Fron, and smiling. She had found him. He'd treated her scalded ankle in A&E then thrown up in a bedpan with the winter vomiting bug.

Who looks after you? she'd asked.

He'd sent her a bunch of nettles the next day. Broken the rules, found her address. You've stung me, the card said.

Later, he tells her where they can go. Fron, he says, where he's from. Hills like breasts. Fog like a beast. He holds onto her shoulders as he convinces her. Sucks on her like a child.

And then she sees him. He's there, just up ahead in a field, and he holds onto a little girl's hand. She is skipping. She wears wellington boots. Her hair, she swears, is pure gold. He bends down with her to look at something in the grass.

She stops the car.

They are picking nettles. It is a field of nettles they cannot feel. And the nettles will all be for her.

She drives back to the little cottage sinking deeper into fog under the hill. She repacks the car and leaves him no note. She is not sorry and has no regrets. As she drives past the field she sees him still there and this time he turns and waves.

She tells herself: there was no scalded foot. No dead mouse in the kettle, and the clocks had all stopped for the Connollys up in Fron as the smoke filled each little room and took their lives one by one. He had gone home as they had all gone home. His mother's last Christmas, the father long gone; three brothers. The sister. To draw up a contract. To say their goodbyes. None of them ever meant to set this world alight.

It's freezing in here, Mother. Light the fire.

It's not that cold, Michael. Put a jumper on. Anyway, I think the seal's gone.

The sister mocks: And you're the one who wants to live in this place?

I do.

You won't survive the night.

That's why I'm lighting the fire.

Don't light the fire, Michael. Please don't light the fire.

Too late.

But the fire burned much later.

She stops the car. This must be it. It has to be it. For there is the view and there is the little cottage under the hill over there. Where we will start again, he'd said. Just as the road ends.

She lifts the box from the well of the passenger seat and heads back towards that nowhere called Fron, scattering him all the way.

Abdul

ON PAPER HE IS a sixteen-year-old Afghan asylum-seeker who has been in the country for three weeks. He made it over on the ferry having been in the Jungle for three months, and there was a passport, relevant documentation. Medical reports have suggested slight symptoms of asthma but no significant trauma. Health otherwise good. He is 1.84 metres in height, weighs just shy of ten stone, statistically speaking he is a human eel, a critically endangered species. Personal belongings: prayer mat, Koran. His name is Abdul. He was born on January 1st 2000 and, like the rest of the millennium bugs that didn't spread, he will slip from the system and have no file.

He is not afraid to look me straight in the eye and, as he does, he shakes my hand though it is all beyond my grasp. I present my ID card—I'm a social worker, that's all—yet he takes me for an official. So the handshake stops and the eyes flick down to the concrete. He seems to be counting pebbles. One pebble. Two pebbles. Takes interest in a slug. I ask for his belongings, what I might put in the car. He carries a white plastic bag like a clutch and unravels it to scoop out what he has. Prayer mat. Koran. Chewing gum. A watch that he straps to his right wrist. He is left-handed and clean-shaven—does he need to shave yet?—and, though he smells like a bathed baby, the air is filled with something so potent I spend a long time trying to place it. The clothes he now wears are donated. The shirt is black and too big. The jeans are old-fashioned. His hair clipped close to his scalp. He leads. I follow. Even from behind he does not look sixteen.

He knows what to do in the car. How to use a seat belt. How to adjust the seat so that he has more leg room. He does not remove his coat. It is October. We are getting sunsets the colour of slit eels. Yet he shivers, this human eel who's slipped into the net; blows into his hands. I turn up the heater. Buckle myself in. I am his chauffeur, I think. Just a cabbie with a fare.

I explain to Abdul that our journey will take around four hours, but given the time of day we are likely to hit Birmingham we could be looking at six. When I use the word traffic I'm really careful not to sound as if it ends with a strong k. I am speaking clearly but not like he's a child and I make no hand gestures to support my words. I notice that there is a scar on his right hand between his thumb and his forefinger; the sort made should you have grabbed a blade to stop it from going any closer to your body. There is also a scar on his neck that looks as recent as the one on his hand. He's already been hooked up and fresh skin has yet to heal his wounds.

When I say his name, he doesn't seem to hear it, nor does he care for my thoughts on rural Kent. I have not been to Afghanistan so we share no common ground, and I regret not making a list of things to talk about. Moving does not suit me either, I want to say. In fact, the older I get, the less of the world I want to see. I turn on the car radio while I'm thinking of what to say. Abdul jumps out of his skin and sheds it. I watch it slip into the gulley of the passenger seat and start to ferment under the heater. Eels can swim backwards you know, I want to say. So you're going to have to get a grip else they'll throw you back into the sea.

Except he is telling *me* something. The Taliban smash car windows to remove car radios is what he is trying to tell me with his fists. And the music here is shit, he says.

He pulls out a mobile phone. There is something he wants to show me. He turns down the radio.

This my music, he says. We have at weddings.

For the first time I wonder if he's married. If that marriage has also borne a child.

We listen to his music as if dancing around each other, avoiding the other one's eyes.

So, I say. You were three months in the Jungle.

He looks out of the window.

Were you there by yourself? With family? Friends?

He is still looking out of the window.

Can I ask how you got there? To the Jungle?

I walk, he says.

That's a long walk, I say. A very long walk.

Yes, he agrees. Very long.

No boat? Truck? Just walking?

Yes, he says again. Just walk.

Once they've crossed the Channel, they are nine times out of ten taken to a warehouse facility in rural Kent where they are kept. Which is how everyone speaks of it. As if they are asking you to keep the change. Which makes me think of the pound. He's being kept in Kent, they will say, while councils wrangle over who's having who. After the tests and assessments determine their truths and their lies in these austere times. After their clothes are incinerated and their lives stripped bare. And it should *not* matter. It should not matter. And I realise that was the smell I was trying to place. Burning fabric. A mass cremation of the clothes off their backs.

We give you money for more clothes, I say.

In Birmingham? he asks. He says it as if it's spelt with an 'a' and not an 'i' when he cannot use the 'I' when he's to become one of them.

We're not going to Birmingham, I say. We only pass through Birmingham but do not stop. You can buy clothes in Stoke. Tomorrow. A translator will take you shopping. For food. For clothes.

Things he will like. Things that will give him back his I.

Abdul is thinking about this. He has a very defined jawbone, long drawn out cheeks. His eyes are flecked with the sort of brown you associate with a stray hound.

Not Birmingham? he asks.

No, I say. Stoke. Near Birmingham.

I have no map. I should've brought a map. Blankets. Food. More kindness.

How far the Birmingham? he asks.

He is agitated. His eyebrows knit. He clenches fists. I tell him one hour.

One hour? he repeats. Because time is everything. It's all he has.

Yes, I say. Birmingham is one hour from Stoke. Where we are going.

He says this over and over. One hour. One hour. Like a mantra. Like something he must not forget.

I have been driving since 4.30 a.m. It is almost noon and I am hungry. So when I see that the next service station is three miles away, I tell Abdul that we will stop. For food. To use the bathroom.

One hour, is how he replies.

At the services I call Christie while I wait for Abdul to return from the bathroom. She has just got up. She yawns. Is drinking coffee. She has all the time in the world and has no idea what to do in it. She is this. She is that. She's going to jack that in to do this again.

Have you got him? she asks. What's he like? Is he old? Does he speak much English?

He's frightened, I say, then remind her to put out the bins. That will give her something to do.

We stand side by side in the service station, Abdul and I, looking at the fast food. I point to the pictures. I have no idea of the Afghan diet. Like I have not thought of anything I should have to make him feel at home. Abdul points to McDonald's.

That, he says, and we join the queue.

There are three girls and a boy in front of us. Teenagers tethered to mobile phones in sweat clothes and trainers. Abdul watches them but not with any interest. He is not looking at the girls in any way that might suggest he has been lonely. He does not look at the boy with envy, distrust or longing. He just looks at them. And as he looks, I realise just how tired he is. And disappointed. As if it's not been worth it. Though he does, in a blink-and-you'll-miss-it moment, look at their trainers. Which makes me for the first time look down at his shoes. Which they are. They are black loafers with rubber soles. The sort teenagers wouldn't be seen dead in.

We find an empty table and sit down with our trays. Abdul spends some time looking about the place. At first, I think he is surveying it and for the first time since I picked him up it crosses my mind that he might be checking things out. You know, like *checking things out*. But then I realise, as he checks his watch, that he is checking the place out because of the time and he would, if still back home, be called to prayer.

There is no prayer room here, I say quietly. Sorry.

And I am, because I didn't think about that. So I say it again. Sorry.

But Abdul is looking at his burger as if it is smothered with flies and this is not the land of everything after all.

I ask Abdul a few questions while we eat. He tells me his father and mother still live and are farmers. He is the only boy. There are three sisters. One is already married. The other two will be soon. If they're lucky. And he says no more than that. I am quiet, sifting through questions that go no further than the tip of my tongue until he tells me in very good English that his family are good people and his village is full of good people. There are no bad, he tells me. But it is hell.

I nod. There is nothing else I can do or say to that.

Abdul is a slow eater. Occasionally, he brings a napkin to his mouth. Then he pushes the napkin into his jacket pocket.

Would you like something different to eat? I ask.

It occurs to me that he is struggling to digest it all so I say that I'm going to get a newspaper. But I'm also wanting to see if he's being looked at. If people really are as antagonistic as the headlines make out. But no one looks. No one is interested. Everyone is mid journey. Just like him.

Back in the car and Abdul is more chatty. It starts with the news on Radio 2. There's been a sports bulletin and he listens to it then asks me of the cricket. He plays. For the under-twenty-fives. He's a fast bowler. He lifts his right arm to show me how his elbow juts a certain way for a spin he is known for.

We can find you a cricket team, I say. Somewhere to play.

English school? he asks.

That too, I say.

Tomorrow?

I do a weird motion with my head as if there is something stuck in my back teeth.

Not tomorrow, I say. But soon.

I start the English, he says, and there's that urgency again.

Tomorrow is Saturday, I tell him. The weekend. No school. No work. I sort it all out on Monday.

Too late, he says. I start tomorrow. English lesson.

No, I say. There is no school tomorrow. I have to sort it out for you. On Monday.

Monday too late, he says and he is angry.

I'm sorry, Abdul, I say. But it doesn't work like that. I will sort it all out for you, I promise. But tomorrow is Saturday. The weekend. You understand? I will get everything sorted out for you next week.

He punches the dashboard. I instantly brake hard which throws us both forward. For a moment I'm winded—as if he's punched me—and I wonder if I should pull over. Instead, I say sorry again and stare straight ahead. It has never occurred to me before just how straight motorways are and that I really do drive too slow for the middle lane as Christie always complains.

There's a hold-up. Car hazards flash—Abdul covers his eyes—and I slow down. One hour to Birmingham and he must learn English by tomorrow.

Must be an accident, I say, as Abdul keeps his head down like he's expecting to drive past the dead.

It too slow, he mutters at his knees.

So I lean over Abdul to get to the glovebox and pull out some CDs. I hand them to him.

Anything you like?

He looks down at the pile of CDs I've dropped onto his lap.

No, he says. He hasn't looked at any of them.

Fair enough, I say, and I take the CDs and choose one. I'm partial to a bit of Queen—Christie despises Queen—play a greatest hits and whack up the volume. We listen to 'We Will Rock You' and 'Radio Ga Ga' and Abdul watches me drumming on the steering wheel.

You know Queen? I ask.

He shakes his head.

I know this. Abdul turns down the volume and starts to sing.

Sing. Sing a song. Sing of good things not bad. Sing of happy not sad.

I sing along with him, smiling. Mainly because he has let go of the fists.

The Carpenters, I say. You know that?

Yes, he says. My mother sing. A hundred per cent singing it all a bloody time.

Then he laughs. Like, really laughs, like the first time he's laughed in ages and it almost chokes him. I flick through the CDs again.

218

No Carpenters, I tell Abdul. Sorry.

No Carpenters, he repeats, and he turns to look out of the window, watches a couple of crisp packets giddy in the wind, then tells me with a lump in his throat, No Carpenters. Not any more.

We get going again but the traffic is bumper to bumper most of the way up to Birmingham. As we go past Coventry and hit signs for Birmingham West and City Centre, I wonder if I should tell Abdul that this *is* Birmingham—we are in Birmingham—I went to university in Birmingham, met Christie in Birmingham, fell in love in Birmingham—and whether I should just drive him to where he wants to be. Because all I am doing is following orders—like he is probably following the orders of whomever has brought him over here, because this has cost him. This life I am driving him to will be expensive. Illegal. I can see where the leeches have already begun to suck. So as the traffic starts to clear I put my foot down and don't even mention to Abdul that over there is Birmingham where he's been sold a lie far bigger than where we are headed.

Abdul says he needs to pee. We are coming up to Junction 14 on the M6 and I know there's another service station just up ahead so I tell him we can use the bathroom there. Part of me wonders if this is the plan and this is the service station where he'll be picked up and taken back to Birmingham, where he'll wash cars or manage dope farms and never be within spitting distance of seeing his family again. But the other part of me, the one who is following government orders, decides that Abdul just needs to pee.

Yet at the service station, Abdul tells me he needs to pray. I don't make any suggestion as to where he might go but he takes himself off, to a patch of grass where the dogs cock their legs and their owners leave their shit behind. He rolls out his mat and looks up at what's left of the sun.

Some people watch him but mostly he's ignored. I hope that's what happens for him when he gets to Birmingham. That he's just allowed to do whatever he needs to do.

I head for the car. When I look back at Abdul I see he is running. I dump the coffees on the roof of the car and call out at the top of my voice. Then I start to run. But he is just chasing his carrier bag that has blown away in the slightest breeze. He looks at me. I look at him. I don't say sorry. And I will regret that.

Back in the car he feels less slippery. So I explain what will happen next and talk as if he understands every word.

That he has a room in the YMCA where he will live. For now.

That he will have a little money to buy clothes and food.

That a translator will take him shopping. Perhaps introduce him to other Afghans.

That he must inform the YMCA if he is going out so he can be checked back in.

That we will talk about enrolling him in a school on Monday, about his wishes, his feelings, and cricket.

I keep on talking as we drive through Stoke as if I need to keep him distracted, so I am still talking when we pull up at the YMCA and I tell him I have a TV for him, in the boot of my car. He looks at me as if he cannot believe his luck. Then says, no TV. Please. It is not what he needs. And he goes to ask me something but here is Karen fumbling about with keys and the right keys, and then we are hurried into an office to sign the paperwork because we are late, Karen says, and she's got to get home. And as Abdul is asked to sign right there and is handed a single key, he breaks down.

Abdul

As Abdul sobs, I put my hand briefly on his shoulder as if I understand. I don't. And I never will.

The room is basic, student digs really, fairly clean but fine, though the flimsy set of curtains don't meet in the middle and Abdul will be too tall to fit the bed. He feeds a duvet its cover, does the same with a pillowcase, shakes out a fitted sheet, then spends a long time looking down at the bed as I connect up the TV. I know he will not sleep in it. That he will instead set up camp on the floor and curl into a space he is used to. I hand him the remote and we flick through a few channels. It is gone 8 p.m. and I'm so exhausted, I find that I am apologising for the TV ads.

I have to go soon, I tell him, but I can't quite leave him yet. So I start rifling through the food parcel to give him an idea of the things he might be able to eat over the weekend.

Cornflakes for breakfast, I instruct. Milk here. I'll put it in the fridge for you. And there's bread. A toaster is here, see? You've pasta, tomato sauce, and there's rice.

I laugh at the packet of dried mixed herbs and tell him to add lots for flavour. I show him a tin of rice pudding. A family bag of crisps. He sits on the bed across from me and just stares.

Anything else you'd like to know? I ask, and he is shivering. I'm in a fairly thick jumper still warm from the car's heater so I take it off and give it to him. I tell him I will see him on Monday. He puts on the jumper and looks up at me and though he says nothing, I know I will never see Abdul again because this isn't the life he has bought.

Abdul wasn't there when I went back on Monday. Karen said she hadn't seen him for most of Saturday then on Sunday he'd complained of a fever and gone back to bed. He'd been shopping with the translator, visited the mosque, and had also asked for directions to the train station. As Karen continued to discuss Abdul like a disobedient dog who has just cost her a fortune at the vet's, I excused myself to go up to his room. Everything was the same as I'd left it on Friday, except there on the bed was my jumper. I immediately put it on as I'd not brought a coat and my blood had suddenly gone cold.

Original sources

'Barmouth' was shortlisted for the BBC Short Story Award 2013, broadcast on BBC Radio 4, 2013, and published by Comma Press, 2013.

'Dirty Laundry' was first published on *www.shortstorysunday.co.uk*, on January 4th 2015.

'Broken Crockery' won *The Guardian*'s National Short Story Competition, August 2009.

'The Cherry Tree' first appeared as part of the online anthology *The Casual Electrocution of Strangers*, a project by Literary Salmon, October 2015.

'Johnny Dangerously' first appeared in *The New Welsh Review*, March issue, 2014.

'The Land of Make Believe' was Highly Commended in the Bridport Prize 2015, and published in the *Bridport Prize* anthology, Redcliffe Press. 'Hoops' made the longlist in 2016.

'Chuck and Di' first appeared in *Hidden Voices* anthology for *The Luminary*, September 2014.

'The Trees in the Wood' was commissioned by Comma Press for their *Spindles: The Science of Sleep* collection undertaken with the Wellcome Trust in 2015.

'Fron' was longlisted for the BBC Short Story Award 2018.

'Abdul' was longlisted for the *Sunday Times* Short Story Award, 2018.

Ta, duck

THERE'S A WHOLE nine years between 'Broken Crockery' and 'Abdul' so I'd first like to thank all those I don't know who've read my stories, found my stories, chosen my stories and bought this book. I hope our paths will cross one day for me to shake your hand.

And then to the folk I'm lucky enough to know and who know how much these stories mean: Phil and Becky, Len and Jim, Hallsy, Deb, Ami, Mags and Steve, Petra, Maz, Rachy, Lord and Lady Moncrieff, John and Sandra, Laura Creyke, Siani Hughes, Laura and Lee, Jo and Dan, Anna Dreda, Fay Bailey, Meg Hawkins, Liz Lefroy, Fat Boy, Nick Button, Jack and David, Jim Hawkins, Phil Gillam, and to all the Blowers and the Edwardses with the A53 in between.

To Philippa Brewster who has been my word glue from the word go and continues to always believe in me and my stories. To Candida Lacey and the Myriad team, who also saw something in me to give me a shot. Thank you x

To Professors Ian Davidson, Helen Wilcox and Ailsa Cox— for their tireless readings of a novel that never made it but became some of these stories all the same.

To Professor Deborah Wynne and Dr Catherine Burgass for flying that Midlands flag for me.

To my fabulous colleagues at Bangor University—for your support, advice, boiling kettles, listening ears, and allowing me to be me.

To Liz Allard, Justine Willett, Rebekah Staton and Jacqueline Redgewell, who brought 'Barmouth' and 'Pot Luck' to such life.

To the literary wizard Jonathan Davidson and the Room 204 cohort who never cease to amaze.

To Natasha Carlish—thank you for sticking your neck out for me.

To Tania Harrison—a constant shining star.

To the huge talents that are Niall Griffiths, Luke Wright, Hollie McNish, and my short fiction consciousness Paul McVeigh. Thank you for reading me and always being so supportive.

To Kit de Waal. Where do I even start? x

To Ra Page at Comma Press for always giving me a chance to be part of a project that blows me away.

To the team behind Literary Salmon—Jane Roberts, Fran Harvey, Alexa Radcliffe-Hart—and to Cathy Galvin and the Word Factory team for always keeping me in mind.

Finally, to my mum, dad and Sarah, who never ever stop listening or thinking I can't do it, and to Dave who reads me better than anyone and puts big light on when I need it.

This book is also in the memory of 'Uncle' Dave Jones. Thank you for mending so many paths going up x

Sign up to our mailing list at
www.myriadeditions.com
Follow us on Facebook and Twitter

About the author

LISA BLOWER is an award-winning writer. Her debut novel *Sitting Ducks* (Fair Acre Press) was shortlisted for the inaugural Arnold Bennett Prize 2017. She is a creative writing lecturer at Bangor University, where she studied for her PhD. She lives in Shrewsbury.